TAKEN

by the

HIGHLANDER

TAKEN

by the

HIGHLANDER

Julianne MacLean

Books by
Julianne MacLean

The American Heiress Series
To Marry the Duke
An Affair Most Wicked
My Own Private Hero
Love According to Lily
Portrait of a Lover
Surrender to a Scoundrel

The Pembroke Palace Series
In My Wildest Fantasies
The Mistress Diaries
When a Stranger Loves Me
Married By Midnight
A Kiss Before the Wedding
(A Pembroke Palace Short Story)
Seduced at Sunset

The Highlander Series
The Rebel – A Highland Short Story
Captured by the Highlander
Claimed by the Highlander
Seduced by the Highlander
Return of the Highlander
Taken by the Highlander

The Royal Trilogy
Be My Prince
Princess in Love
The Prince's Bride

Harlequin Historical Romances
Prairie Bride
The Marshal and Mrs. O'Malley
Adam's Promise

Time Travel Romance
Taken by the Cowboy

The Color of Heaven Series
The Color of Heaven
The Color of Destiny
The Color of Hope
The Color of a Dream
The Color of a Memory
The Color of Love
The Color of the Season
The Color of Joy
The Color of Time

Praise for Julianne MacLean's Historical Romances

"MacLean's compelling writing turns this simple, classic love story into a richly emotional romance, and by combining engaging characters with a unique, vividly detailed setting, she has created an exceptional tale for readers who hunger for something a bit different in their historical romances."
—***BOOKLIST***

"You can always count on Julianne MacLean to deliver ravishing romance that will keep you turning pages until the wee hours of the morning."
—**Teresa Medeiros**

"Julianne MacLean's writing is smart, thrilling, and sizzles with sensuality."
—**Elizabeth Hoyt**

"Scottish romance at its finest, with characters to cheer for, a lush love story, and rousing adventure. I was captivated from the very first page. When it comes to exciting Highland romance, Julianne MacLean delivers."
—**Laura Lee Guhrke**

"She is just an all-around wonderful writer, and I look forward to reading everything she writes."
—***Romance Junkies***

PART ONE

The Rescue

CHAPTER

One

The full moon shone high in the inky sky as Logan Campbell emerged out of the forest onto a wide river valley. The pain in his broken arm was so severe, he passed out for a few seconds and didn't realize he'd toppled off his horse.

Landing with a heavy thud on the grass, he immediately regained consciousness, curled up in agony, and clutched his broken arm close to his ribs.

God help him. If he didn't set the bone in place soon, the swelling would make it impossible to do so, and it might never heal properly. This was his sword arm and he couldn't afford to lose it.

He was kicking himself now. He shouldn't have ridden away from the camp in such a fury. He should have at least remained long enough to allow his brother Darach to tend to the bone, but Logan's pride hadn't allowed it—not when Darach had been the one to break his arm in the first place.

Logan supposed he'd had it coming. As usual, he'd started the fight. Over a woman, of course. He had been the first one to draw a blade.

Ach! The pain was insufferable. He couldn't put it off any longer.

Sitting up carefully on the grass, Logan reached into his boot for his knife and placed the well-worn, wooden grip between his teeth. He then felt along the length of his fore-arm, pressing as gently as possible with his thumb to locate the break, but he couldn't find it through the rigid swelling of his flesh. He had to press more firmly. Suddenly, an acute pain exploded just above his wrist and he knew he'd found the spot.

Bloody hell, what he wouldn't give for a bottle of whisky...

Biting down hard on the handle of the knife, he rammed all his grip-strength into resetting the bone.

Snap!

Pain shot through his body like a massive cannon ball, from his wrist straight up to his brain where it reverberated against his skull. His thunderous, agonized roar echoed from one side of the glen to the other, then he collapsed onto his back where he lay for a long time, gazing up at the stars. Waiting wretch-edly for the agony to subside, he wondered what he would use to bind his arm in place—if he ever found the strength and fortitude to rise to his feet.

What was his brother doing now? Logan wondered in a daze.

Darach had probably packed up the camp and taken their hostage somewhere safe. A place where Logan couldn't find her or use her as a pawn to gain entry into Leathan Castle—the Campbell stronghold that had once been Logan's home. *Their* home, as brothers, many years back.

That's what had been at the root of their quarrel a few short hours ago. Darach hadn't wanted to use the Campbell lass for their own purposes. He'd simply wanted to deliver her through the gates of Leathan and be done with it, for that had been their mission from the outset. It was what the MacDonald Chief had commanded them to do: *Escort Larena Campbell home, for she is the chief's daughter...*

But Logan had made the mistake of entertaining other plans for the lass—for he wanted to kill her father, that murderous Highlander who never had the right to become chief in the first place. That right belonged to Logan's own father, or now that he was dead, the position of chief should have passed to Logan's older brother, Darach.

But Darach had no interest in leading the Campbells of Leathan. He had laid their heritage to rest a long time ago. Buried it good and deep in the ground, far away—in MacDonald territory.

For what seemed like an eternity, Logan listened to the crickets chirping in the grass all around him. The creatures of the night kept a steady rhythm, which seemed to match the throbbing sensation in his arm, although the pain grew hazier with every moment that passed.

Or perhaps it was his thoughts that were growing hazy as he fell into a deep slumber, where all of this was naught but a bad dream.

⁂

It was the sound of the man's agonized cry that woke Mairi Campbell from sleep. At least that's what she thought it was as she sat up in bed with a racing heart, searching through the darkness with wide eyes. The fire in the hearth was long dead, so she reasoned it was well past midnight—an odd time to hear a man bellowing in the glen.

But of course, she had been dreaming. It wasn't the first time she'd dreamed of a man's agonized cries—perhaps as a mallet came down on his hand or as he was pushed over the side of a steep cliff. But those days were over. She was no longer a woman who imagined such vengeful things.

Tossing the covers aside and rising from her small bed, she went to check on her son, Hamish. He had fallen asleep in her mother's bed earlier that evening after a special treat of sweet custard and raspberries in celebration of his fifth birthday.

Watching over him, as he slept close to his grandmother in a loving embrace, Mairi marveled at how quickly the years had flown by. It seemed only yesterday that Hamish spoke his first words or took his first wobbly steps outside in the stable yard.

Today he was five, which meant the time had come to be more diligent in teaching him to read. Mairi wanted that for him more than anything, so he would have options in life. Perhaps there was a chance he would not choose to live by the sword. If she had her druthers, Hamish would grow up to be an educated crofter like his grandfather, and live in peace.

Backing out of her mother's room, Mairi padded across the plank floor to the kitchen, lit a candle and poured herself a small cup of wine, for she couldn't seem to purge the disturbing dream from her mind. She kept hearing the intensity of the man's pain, over and over, as if someone were holding him over the scorching flames of hell.

She shuddered at the thought, and yet a part of her felt shame at the recollection of how she'd imagined similar images countless times—but it was no faceless man who had suffered in her imaginings.

It was Captain Joseph Kearney. English officer, handsome enough to get away with murder. And other despicable things.

But that was a long time ago. In another life. She should not think of it now, for she was the luckiest woman in the world to have Hamish as her son. That was all that mattered—the present and the future—not the past.

As she raised the cup to her lips, she smiled at the thought of Hamish's excitement earlier that day when their neighbor and friend, Tomas Campbell, had ridden into the yard and presented him with a small toy horse he'd carved himself. She had never heard Hamish squeal with such delight before.

With a calmer heart, Mairi sat down at the table. She had just taken a second sip of wine when the sound of a horse nickering in the field behind the cottage caused her to rise to her feet again. At first she thought she might have imagined it, even dreamed it, but there it was again.

There could be no mistaking it. This was no midnight dream. Someone was outside in the darkness.

Setting down her cup, she hastened to her bed, donned a skirt and bodice over her shift, pulled on her boots, and sheathed her dirk in the leather uppers. Then she fetched her father's pistol from the box under the bed—*her* pistol now. She loaded it quickly and expertly, and tiptoed through the cottage to the front door.

Lifting the latch, she pulled the door open a mere crack to peer around the moonlit yard. Seeing no one about, she exited the house and sidled along the stone wall to move around to the back.

Sure enough, when she peered around the corner, she saw something—a riderless, bare-backed horse, beneath the luminescent glow of the moon, nibbling grass.

Mairi took a breath and glanced around in all directions, listening keenly for any sounds or movements. Seeing or hearing none, she cautiously approached the animal.

"Do not be afraid," she whispered. "I will not hurt you."

He lifted his head, watched her for a moment, then strode closer to meet her.

"Who do you belong to?" she asked as she stroked the firm muscles at his neck. "Are you lost?"

He tossed his head and nickered.

Recalling yet again the distressing sound of a man's cry that woke her from her sleep, she felt a shiver move up her spine.

Perhaps someone needed help—in which case she had a moral duty to investigate and offer assistance. If there was some other explanation for the agonizing sound in the night and it involved foul play, she would not be afraid to use her weapon. She had made it her mission five years ago to learn how to protect herself—swearing never to be anyone's victim again. And now she had a son to protect.

Keeping her wits about her, she led the horse into the yard, placed him in their stable and closed the door. Then cautiously, she returned to the field to search the surrounding area.

⋘⊹⋙

Logan's eyes flew open at the sound of a pistol cocking.

It was the second time that night he'd been approached by someone with a gun. Last time, it had been his brother and all hell had broken loose.

Pray God, this would yield different results, for Logan was in no mood—or condition—for another round of fisticuffs. He was in such pain, he didn't even try to get up. In that moment he'd almost prefer to take the pistol ball straight between the eyes.

Still lying flat on his back, he craned his neck to look up and found himself gazing at a woman—a comely looking woman with dark hair and ivory skin that gleamed in the silvery light of the moon.

"I see you're a MacDonald," she said, taking in the colors of his tartan and the polished brooch he wore.

Nay, he was not a MacDonald. He was a Campbell by blood, but if anyone ever discovered his true identity, there would be a price on his head for sure.

So he did what he always did. He lied.

"Aye," he replied. "I come from Kinloch Castle. I'm a scout for Angus the Lion." That part was true, at least.

She scowled at him. "The Great Lion of Kinloch? What the devil are you doing in Campbell territory, looking like you've been beaten to a pulp? Or perhaps I should be asking another question. Why were you shouting so foolishly in the middle of the night, giving away your location?"

"My arm is broken," he explained, feeling wretched, weary and sick. All the fight had gone out of him. "I had to set the bone. It smarted."

The lass glanced down at his bruised and swollen forearm, which he held close to his chest. "No doubt. Are you alone?"

"Aye."

She quickly surveyed the area. "How did you break it?"

Since he knew nothing about this woman or from where she came, he decided another lie was in order. "I fell asleep and toppled off my horse."

For a long moment she kept her weapon trained on his head—as if she were scrutinizing the cuts and bruises on his face where Darach had punched him repeatedly. Then she moved around him to stand at his feet, where the moon illuminated her face and he could see her better.

Lord help him. Now that he was awarded a better view, his body stirred with sexual awareness, for she was far more beautiful than he'd first realized—one of the most striking women he'd ever encountered. She had a shiny mane of thick dark hair that fell in long, tousled waves over her shoulders to frame a captivating heart-shaped face. Her chocolate-brown eyes were enormous and penetrating. And by God, those lips...like sweet, juicy cherries, full and ripe, were perfect for kissing. It caused his mouth to water.

Perhaps he should have had more sense under the circumstances, but his body was in such upheaval—trying to process both pain and desire—that he forgot himself. His gaze dipped to her lush bosom, where he spent a considerable number of seconds admiring her sensual feminine endowments. Then he glanced lower still, to her tiny waist and delectably curvy hips.

The lass took a purposeful step forward, aimed the pistol between his eyes, and spoke through gritted teeth. "I'm warning you..."

Wrenched violently from his reverie, Logan's thoughts returned to the acute throbbing in his arm. He blinked a few times and swallowed. "Apologies. I meant no disrespect and I pose no threat to you. I swear I'm in no condition to cause trouble."

"Give me one good reason why I should believe anything you say," she argued. "What about tomorrow when you're feeling better?"

He sighed heavily. "I suspect this arm won't be much good to me for quite some time."

"Is it your fighting arm?" she asked, matter-of-factly.

"Aye."

A tense moment of indecision ensued while she considered her options. At long last, she released the pistol's hammer and lowered it to her side. "You'll need a splint."

"Aye."

"I can help you," she said, "but only if you answer my question. What's a MacDonald scout doing on Campbell lands? Our two clans are not exactly on friendly terms, as you well know. More importantly, what are you doing on my *father's* property?"

"Who's your father?" Logan asked hazily, doubting he could even process her reply, whatever it might be.

"No one important, and I'll be the one asking the questions."

Letting his eyes fall closed, Logan nodded. "Whatever you wish, lass. I've not the strength or inclination to argue with you. I just want the pain to go away."

⁂

Mairi stood with a pounding heart, watching the MacDonald scout wince as he tried to sit up. Part of her was thankful he was injured, for he was a powerful-looking man—tall and broad shouldered with thick, solid muscles and an unsettlingly self-assured air about him, considering the situation.

Perhaps it was his looks that had instilled such confidence in him. Aside from the fact that he had a fat lip and a few scrapes across his cheek, he was compellingly handsome with golden hair, chiseled features, and green eyes that blinked up at her with a boyish charm—the type of charm that could easily melt a woman's defenses.

A dangerous attribute, to be sure, for if he was a scout for Angus the Lion, he was also, no doubt, a strong man and a highly skilled warrior. Judging by the way he had taken such liberties with his eyes just now—admiring her body, her bosom especially—he was definitely *not* the sort of man with whom she should let down her guard.

She knew better than most what could come of such imprudence.

Nevertheless, she could not turn her back on the injured Highlander, for she remembered something her father had said to her once—that Scots had to stick together if they ever hoped to triumph over the English. She had made a promise to him that she would never turn a fellow Scot away from her door if he meant her no harm.

"Your color's not good," she informed the stranger in her field. "You look pasty."

Sitting up, with his legs stretched out in front of him, still hugging his arm close to his chest, he lifted those magnetic green eyes and inclined his head apologetically. "I'm afraid I'm not at my best to make your acquaintance, lass. May I ask your name?"

"It's Mairi. Mairi Campbell."

He regarded her intently. "I'm Logan. I would bow upon making your acquaintance, but..." He shrugged and lowered his gaze again.

"This is hardly the time for formalities," she said flatly. "Please, allow me to help you up."

"I can do it," he insisted as he struggled to his feet. Once he found his balance, he paused a moment, then swayed slightly.

Mairi holstered her pistol in the waistband of her skirt but stood ready to catch him if he toppled.

"Aye. Just a bit light-headed," he explained.

"Can you walk? I don't live far from here. It's just over that rise." She pointed in the direction of her home.

Logan squinted into the distance and grimaced slightly. "Aye."

Slowly, she led the way, keeping a close eye on him in case he should lose consciousness and collapse.

Or try to force himself on her.

They walked slowly, side by side. Logan was quiet—focused on managing his pain, no doubt.

After a time, Mairi ventured to ask, "Are you certain you were successful in setting the bone?"

"Aye, I felt it snap into place." He scanned the horizon from left to right. "I don't suppose you've seen my horse? He seems to have abandoned me."

He didn't abandon you," she replied. "You owe him a great debt, in fact. I would never have known to come looking for you if he hadn't strolled into my back field and made his presence known. I put him in the stable, so he's safe for the time being."

Logan let it out a breath. "I believe *you* are the person I owe a debt to, Mairi."

"I haven't done anything yet," she replied curtly.

He slid an engaging glance in her direction and spoke with a hint of flirtation. "You didn't shoot me. That's something."

Mairi ignored his attempt to beguile her. "Only because you've been reasonably well behaved so far."

"But only *reasonably*," he said with a glimmer of playfulness in his eyes, which she also made a point to ignore.

Realizing he was getting nowhere with her, he let out a frustrated breath. "I apologize for how I looked at you earlier. I was in a bit of a daze. I thought maybe I was dreaming, or that you were an angel sent here to escort me to the great beyond."

"I'm no angel," she replied. "And you're not dead. Nonetheless...don't do it again or I might change my mind about shooting you."

She felt him scrutinize her as he nodded. "Understood."

At last, they reached the stable yard and Mairi considered what to do with the injured Highlander. If she brought him into the cottage, she would wake Hamish and her mother. And where would she put him? There were no extra beds, and it would hardly be wise for her to allow a stranger to sleep on the floor in the main room with nothing but a curtain as a barrier between them. Oh, why had she made that promise to her father?

Pausing in the yard, she turned to him. "You'll have to sleep in the stable. I have a young son. I don't wish to wake him. Besides, I don't know you from Adam." She gestured toward the stable. "There's a cot with a down-filled pillow in there. I'll bring you a blanket and something to eat."

"That will be fine, Mairi," he replied. "But if it's all the same to you, I would prefer some whisky or wine. To numb the pain."

"Of course. Please, follow me." She led him to the stable door, opened it, and showed him inside. Moonlight spilled across the dirt floor and the chickens flew into a frenzy at the disruption. She moved to light the lantern. "Your horse is there," she said.

The great beast nickered and tossed his head, as if to express his relief at seeing his master arrive safely.

"You can sleep over there." She pointed at the cot across from the stall where she kept the goats. "But before I leave you for the night, we must put a splint on your arm. I will see what I have in the house that can be of use."

"This is beyond generous," Logan said. He stopped to look around while she hung the lantern on a peg on the center post. "I cannot thank you enough."

"No need. Please sit down before you fall over. I'll be back soon."

He ambled past the stalls to the cot.

A strange fluttering arose in her belly at the sight of his for-titude—not to mention how handsome he was. It was a novel feeling to be sure, as she rarely, if ever, felt an attraction to men, especially strangers. She generally regarded them with suspicion and contempt.

As she walked out of the stable and returned to the house, she urged herself to remain cautious and not take any chances with her safety, or her son's. She could not forget how he'd looked at her with unconstrained desire in those first few moments in the glen. She knew all too well where that could lead…and the price she would pay for it.

With that in mind, she locked the door securely behind her before searching the cottage for something to use as a splint for the Highlander's arm.

Logan sat down on the cot and breathed deeply a few times to try and quell the thunderous, throbbing sensation in his arm. At least he'd be guzzling whisky soon. That should help. He hoped Mairi would return with a full bottle, because he would dearly love to drink himself into an absolute, dead-to-the-world stupor.

But first he would need to endure the agony of putting his arm in a splint. He hoped the lass would have a gentle touch.

Unfortunately, he didn't hold much store in that.

With a weary sigh of resignation, he thought about lying down, but that would mean he'd have to sit up again, and any such movements were sheer torture. Best to wait for the whisky.

As a result, he had no choice but to sit in the dim lantern light, looking around at the goats in the stall across from his bed and the chickens that roamed about, clucking without a care in the world. There were a number of tools hung on the far wall—a turf spade with a wooden handle, a couple of mallets, an ax, and a harness to use with the wagon and plow he'd noticed outside. But there was no horse in the stable, other than his own.

He wondered where the lassie's father was, or her husband, as she'd mentioned she had a son. Clearly there was no man present in the cottage, else he would have been the one to approach Logan in the field with a loaded pistol.

Just then, the stable door opened and Mairi swept in, carrying a basket full of items. Logan sat up slightly, energized by her return and the expectation that she had brought something potent in a bottle.

She, on the other hand, did not seem happy to be in his presence again. She walked briskly past his horse, Tracker, and dropped the basket down on the cot beside him, then withdrew the bottle of whisky and a small goblet.

"For the pain." She removed the cork with her teeth and poured him a generous amount.

"A lady after my own heart," he replied jauntily as he accepted the drink.

She gave him a dark look of warning.

"I wasn't flirting," he explained. "Just expressing my gratitude."

"You're welcome, then," she coolly replied. "Now drink up so we can get this done."

"Happy to do so." He tossed the whisky back in a single gulp and grimaced at the scalding sensation that opened fire down his gullet. "Aye, that's good," he ground out. Holding the cup out again, he waited for her to refill it. "To your health," he said before gulping it down. "*Ach*, that's really good stuff."

"It should be. It's Moncrieffe Whisky. We've had it in the house for ages."

Logan's head drew back slightly. "Now I feel *beyond* grateful, lass. Should you be wasting your best bottle on a stranger in your stable for only one night?"

She shrugged indifferently. "I have no other use for it."

Her cool response aroused his curiosity as she rifled through the basket and withdrew two small wooden planks and strips of

cloth. She measured the length of the planks against his fore-
arm. "This will do. Roll up your sleeve."

Still waiting for the whisky to take effect, he began the
assignment rather clumsily, as he was right-handed.

"Let me do it," Mairi said.

She turned her body to face him, and while she rolled the
fabric up to his elbow, he snuck the opportunity to admire her
features more closely. He took in her soft, dewy complexion
and her upturned nose. And those lips...still looking as delicious as they'd appeared in the glen. Her husband was one
lucky man.

"What happened to your leg?" she asked. "You're bleeding
a bit."

He glanced down at the top of his calf. "*Ach*, I hadn't
noticed."

He decided not to mention that on top of everything else,
he was grazed by a musket ball.

She reached for the splints. "Now, hold out your arm and I
will tie these two pieces of wood together to prevent the bone
from separating again. Then we'll fashion a sling for you—to
keep the limb from swinging about."

"It won't be easy to ride," Logan mentioned, fighting to
resist the urge to lean a little closer and breathe in the clean,
delectable scent of her hair. She must have bathed in rosewater
that very night.

"You can cross that bridge when you come to it," she said,
holding the planks out to determine which one to use on either
side of his forearm. "And you never answered my question earlier. Why were you crossing my father's land with nothing but
the clothes on your back? You had no weapons or food, and
your horse wasn't even saddled."

Bracing himself for another onslaught of pain, Logan decided he might as well come clean, for he was no minstrel. He couldn't possibly come up with an elaborate explanation for his plight.

"If you really must know," he replied, "I didn't exactly tell you the truth before."

Her eyes lifted and she reached for the strips of cloth which she'd set on her lap. "I cannot say I'm surprised."

At the meeting of their eyes, a pleasant wave of heat moved through him. Maybe it was the whisky. Maybe not. "I didn't actually fall off my horse," he said. "I'm a better rider than that."

"Go on."

One of the chickens strolled by, clucking softly, pecking at the dirt.

Logan watched Mairi's face as she further considered the best position for the splints. "I quarreled with my brother earlier," he explained. "We were on a mission for our laird, but I wanted to disobey our orders and handle things my own way. We got into a fight over it and I drew my blade—a rash move, I realize now. He did what he had to do and tried to shoot me in the leg. Then he snapped my arm."

"Your own brother?"

"Aye. It was...*complicated*." He paused. "There was a woman involved."

"Ah."

"After that," Logan continued, "I was boiling mad—as you can well imagine—and I rode out of the camp. I didn't even take the time to saddle my horse...not that I could have, at any rate. Not with a broken arm. So that's what happened. I must have passed out from the pain when I fell off my horse in your field."

Mairi regarded him shrewdly. "So that explains the fat lip and the scrapes and bruises on your knuckles. What was the mission?"

Logan's heart began to pound because he had never told *anyone* the truth about who they were and how they'd ended up masquerading as members of the MacDonald clan, much less what Logan had wanted to do during their mission over the past few days—to waltz into the Campbell stronghold with the chief's daughter, explain to the chief exactly who they were so he could contemplate his sins on his way to hell, then march into the powder magazine and blow the whole place into the clouds. Redcoats and all.

"I cannot say."

For a long moment she stared at him in the golden lamp-light, and he found himself forgetting about vengeance and murder...wishing only that he was not so incapacitated and in need of a nursemaid. He hated to appear weak in front of any-one—especially a beautiful woman.

Mairi narrowed her eyes. "So you were just *accidentally* passing through..."

"That's right."

She returned her attention to the task of wrapping his arm. "I'll need you to hold this one in place. Just like that. If you could hold this one as well and cup them together with your good hand...Right, like that." She picked up the strips of cloth. "I'll tie them in place now. Hold steady."

She wrapped the long length of linen around the splints, secured them tightly, and tied the ends. "There." She sat back and examined her work. "How does that feel?"

He couldn't speak for a moment, for it had taken every ounce of self-control he possessed not to utter a few indecent oaths during the unavoidable twisting and turning of his arm.

"Fine," he managed to grind out as he clenched his teeth together.

Mairi reached for the whisky bottle and poured him another glass. "Take this."

He grabbed for it with his good hand and quickly tossed it back. "Another?" he asked.

"I hope we didn't aggravate the break," she said as she poured. "If we did, we'll need to reset it."

"It's still in place," he replied. "It's just sore, that's all. I'll survive." He took the cup of whisky, but held it on his lap for a moment while he collected himself.

Finally, warmth from the whisky flooded his senses and the pain lost some of its intensity. He tipped his head back, closed his eyes, and exhaled with relief.

"I'm afraid we're not quite done yet," Mairi said. "I need to fashion a sling for you. You might want to sleep with it tonight, just to keep from tossing your arm about." She reached into the basket and withdrew a larger section of cloth, then stood up to wrap it under his arm and over his shoulder where she tied a knot.

"You'll feel better tomorrow," Mairi said, setting the basket on the floor. "Then you can be on your way and find your brother. Try to get some sleep."

"Thank you, Mairi," Logan said, lifting his gaze to look up at her. "I appreciate what you've done for me."

"You're welcome." She turned to leave. "Good night."

"Good night," Logan replied, watching her walk out of the stable and close the door behind her. When he looked down, he noticed that she'd left the bottle of whisky for him, still in the basket. He was thankful for that.

Her husband was a fortunate man indeed.

⊱≋⊰

Mairi walked quickly back to the house, shut the door behind her, and locked it securely. She wasn't sure why her heart was racing in her chest or why her belly was pitching and rolling with nervous knots. Was it fear of a strange man in the stable, or something else?

With more than a little unease, she suspected it was the latter, for she hadn't felt anything quite like this in a very long time. More than five years to be exact. Never did she imagine she'd know that feeling again, but how could she help it? He was so wickedly, unbelievably handsome.

Good Lord. What was this?

She must be exceedingly careful.

Swallowing hard, she darted her gaze to the table under the window. Before she knew what she was about, she was dragging the table across the floor and shoving it up against the door, just in case the lock wasn't strong enough to keep Logan out. When she had the table in place and stepped back to examine her handiwork, she raked her fingers through her hair.

Mairi, you're mad! He's not going to burst into the cottage like a brute. He's a wounded, weary man with a broken arm.

Nevertheless, she knew without a doubt that she was going to have a devil of a time getting any rest.

Picking up the candlestick, she tiptoed into her mother's room and pulled the curtain aside to check on her and Hamish.

At first they appeared to be asleep, but then her mother sat up and squinted at Mairi, who held the candle aloft.

"What's going on?" Mother whispered. "I heard you coming and going. Dragging furniture across the room."

"Do not be concerned," Mairi replied, "but there's a man in the stable. He's a Scot. A MacDonald from Kinloch Castle."

Her mother sat up with obvious apprehension.

"He's wounded," Mairi explained. "He broke his arm and needed help. I put a splint on it and gave him some whisky to numb the pain."

Hamish stirred and sat up.

Mairi held her finger to her lips. "*Shhh*, my sweet boy. Go back to sleep."

He snuggled down next to his grandmother and fell into a deep slumber almost immediately.

"Is he alone?" her mother asked in a whisper.

"Aye, and he's no threat tonight. He's in a great deal of pain."

"Good," she replied, then shook her head at herself. "Heavens above, that's not what I meant."

"I knew what you meant," Mairi said. "Go back to sleep now. We'll send him on his way tomorrow."

Her mother nodded and lay back down.

Mairi let the curtain fall closed, turned to cross the kitchen toward her own bed on the opposite side of the cottage, and began to unlace her bodice.

ᚦHREE

Logan's eyes fluttered open at the sound of a rooster crowing somewhere outside in the yard. Soft, early morning light poured in through the small window over his cot. Only then did he become aware of the dull ache in his arm. Thoughts and regrets about what had occurred between him and Darach the night before flooded his brain.

"What's *your* name?" a tiny voice asked.

Sucking in a quick breath, Logan leaned up on his good arm to discover a small, red-haired boy with green eyes standing over him. He looked to be about five.

"It's Logan," he replied, squinting into the daylight while his head pounded from the aftereffects of the whisky. "What's yours?"

"Hamish." The boy pointed a finger. "Why do you have wood tied to your arm?"

Logan held it up. "It's called a splint. I broke a bone last night. Right about here." He pointed. "This will help it heal."

Hamish's eyebrows pulled together as he considered that. "Does my ma know you're in here?"

"Aye," Logan replied. "She's the one who tied the splint on my arm. I needed help and she was very kind."

Just then, Mairi ran into the stable.

"Hamish! Come away from there!" She collected the boy and drew him back from the cot where Logan was fighting to sit up. "This man is a stranger," she said in her son's ear. "You remember what I said about strangers. We don't know them. We must always be cautious."

Logan swung his feet to the floor and hugged his sore arm to his ribs. "Your mother's right," he said, wondering why the lass was so exceedingly wary of strangers. "You must be careful around people and things you don't know anything about. But I give you my word I won't harm you." He pointed to his arm. "Even if I wanted to, I couldn't draw a sword or break out a cannon."

Hamish covered his mouth with a hand and giggled. "Where *is* your sword?" he asked.

Logan gave an exaggerated huff of frustration. "I'm afraid I left it behind. I suspect my brother has it, though."

"You have a brother?"

"Aye."

"Older or younger?" Hamish asked.

"Older. Do *you* have a brother?"

Hamish shook his bushy head of hair. "Nay, but I want one. Then we could fight with each other!"

"Hamish!" Mairi scolded. "That's not what brothers are for. And it's time for breakfast." She led the boy to the stable door. "Go and ask Grammy if the porridge is ready."

Hamish ran back to the cottage. Mairi returned to the stall where Logan was rubbing at his temple. She bent to pick up the whisky bottle and shook what was left in the bottom. "I'm surprised. I thought you might have finished it."

"I'm surprised I *didn't*," he replied, "but I fell asleep—feeling no pain, thank you very much."

She set the bottle in the basket and hooked the handle over her arm. "There's food in the kitchen," she said. "You're welcome to come inside and join us for breakfast."

His eyebrows lifted. "Really? You're going to let a danger-ous intruder like me into your home?"

She rolled her shoulders self-consciously. "I realize I must seem overly protective, but we've had some trouble in the past." She turned to go. "My mother makes an excellent porridge and she's rather vain about it. She looked in on you earlier and felt sorry for you. She insisted that you fill your belly before you leave."

"I like your mother already," Logan replied.

Mairi stopped at the door and faced him again. "How is your arm this morning?"

"Better," he replied, "but my head's not so good. That whisky kicks like a bull."

She chuckled. "Aye. That's why it's been in the house for so long. Dangerous stuff. Best to be avoided."

"Your husband doesn't partake?" He waited eagerly for her reply.

She hesitated. "I have no husband."

Ah, no husband...

"What about your father?"

She lifted her chin and spoke with a coldness in her eyes. "He died five years ago. It's just me and my mother now—and Hamish, of course."

"I'm sorry to hear that," Logan said, acknowledging her grief and wondering if her father's death was part of the 'trou-ble' she'd mentioned earlier.

Mairi glanced away for a moment, then squared her shoul-ders and adjusted the basket looped on her arm. "The porridge should be ready by now. The creek is that way if you'd like to wash up. I'll have a place set for you at the table, but please do not take too long. Hamish is always famished in the mornings. Besides, it looks like rain."

Logan stood. "I'll be quick."

Mairi walked out and left Logan standing alone, feeling in a bit of a daze, but not from the whisky.

Mairi had no husband.

Was she a widow, then?

As he walked out of the stable to wash up for breakfast, he found himself desperate to know more about her life and what had happened to her father and husband...if there ever was one.

For some reason, this woman intrigued him like no other.

⚜

"Good morning. You must be Logan." Wiping her hands on her apron, Mairi's mother greeted Logan at the door with a warm smile. "I'm Isla. Please come in."

Not at all cool and guarded like her daughter, Isla was an attractive older woman with a slim figure, flaxen hair pulled up in a braided knot, and freckles. Logan assumed that Mairi, with her dark coloring, must have taken after her late father.

Isla stepped aside and gestured with a hand for Logan to enter. As he crossed the cottage threshold, he breathed in the delectable scent of hot coffee, and detected a hint of cinnamon as well. It was a glorious balm to his senses after the past few days in the saddle, and for a few pleasant seconds, it helped him forget the throbbing pain in his arm.

He noticed that the table was set for four, with a small cup of wildflowers in the center. A small iron stew pot hung from a hook over the fire in the stone hearth.

Mairi appeared from behind a curtain to a back room and perused him with those stunning dark eyes. The sight of her caused a rush of heat in his blood.

"Good morning again," he said, fighting to keep his fascination with her in check. Otherwise Mairi and her mother might boot him straight back out the door.

She gave him a reserved glance, then moved to gather Hamish up from the floor by the window where he was playing with a wooden toy horse and rider.

"Up you come, Hamish. It's time to eat."

"Is Logan eating with us, too?" Hamish asked excitedly as he set the toys on the windowsill.

"Aye," Mairi replied, "so we must be on our best behavior, mustn't we?"

Isla escorted Logan to the table and indicated a chair for him to sit upon.

"How is your arm this morning?" she asked him as he sat down.

"Better, thank you," he replied.

Mairi served up a bowl of hot porridge and set it before him. As she leaned over him, he couldn't help but admire how a tendril of her dark, wavy hair fell free about her ear, while the rest was swept into a loosely braided knot at the back of her head.

She still smelled of fresh roses, and he had to work hard not to lean even closer to take a deeper breath of her.

Bloody hell. He was a goner.

Mairi poured coffee for everyone and sat down across from Logan. She was so strikingly beautiful in the daylight, it was difficult not to stare.

"Mairi tells me you hail from Kinloch Castle?" Isla said as they all began to eat. "You're a scout for Angus the Lion?"

"That's right," Logan replied.

"What's he like?" Isla asked. "Is he as fierce and monstrous as his reputation makes him out to be?"

"Fierce, aye," Logan replied. "But I would not say monstrous. Perhaps fatherhood has tamed him somewhat since the old days when he was a warrior. From what I know of him, he's as good a chief as any clan could ever want, for we've had nothing but peace and prosperity since he became our laird."

Isla stirred her porridge with her spoon. "I wish we Campbells could say the same. Times have been grim and uncertain in these parts. I presume you've heard what's been happening at Leathan Castle?"

"If you are referring to the invasion by the English army..." Logan replied. "Aye, I've heard of it."

Of course he had. Up until last night, that's precisely where he had been heading.

Isla and Mairi exchanged a look.

"Mairi also tells me you are on some sort of secret mission for your laird," her mother continued. "Dare I ask if it has something to do with the seizure of Leathan by the English?"

Mairi set down her spoon and waited for Logan's response.

He raised some porridge to his lips. "I can tell you this much. I was on my way to Leathan with my brother, on an errand, of sorts. We had a..." He paused. "A *package* to deliver to the Campbell chief."

Isla toyed with her food. "What sort of package could be any good to the chief when he's locked up in his own prison, waiting to go to the gallows?" Her eyes lifted and glimmered with antagonism. "Which is exactly where that Jacobite traitor belongs."

"*Mother...*" Mairi said with a note of warning.

But Logan didn't mind the woman's honesty. In fact, he was growing more and more curious about this small family by the second. "Why would you say that, Isla? Do you not care for the Campbell chief?"

I certainly do not.

Isla gave him a look. "Nay, I do not care for him. Not one wee bit. Do you know he seized control of the castle two years ago when the true and proper laird passed on without any heirs to take his place?"

Of course Logan knew of it—all too well—for he was one of those heirs himself, the youngest son of the late chief. An unknown lost member of the Campbell clan, living his life in hiding at Kinloch Castle, disguised as a MacDonald since the age of eleven. Presumed dead.

"What do you know of the former laird?" Logan asked casually as he spooned some porridge into his mouth.

Isla regarded him intently from across the table. "I know that he was a strong, fair-minded man, and that since his death, the Campbell clan has been divided. There are those who wish to follow their new laird into battle for the Jacobites and those who do not want to rise against the King. And some say the death of our former chief was murder."

Logan made an effort not to flinch, for this was not news to him. In fact, it was why he and Darach had fought so savagely the night before—because Logan wanted vengeance against Fitzroy Campbell, while Darach wanted to lay it all to rest. To leave it in the past and move on. To continue living as scouts for the MacDonalds and never return to their former home or seek revenge.

Nothing can bring our father back, Darach had said. *We are pledged to the MacDonalds now.*

"I heard the former chief's death was an accident," Logan mentioned. "That Ronald Campbell was fatally wounded during a hunt."

"Pure rubbish," Isla replied. "Mark my words...." She waved her spoon at him. "Leathan Castle would *never* have fallen to the English if our true and proper laird had been in charge. That new 'pretender' was a secret Jacobite all along. A traitor to the King—and a foolhardy one at that. He deserved what he got. But the clan certainly didn't. Now the castle has become an English garrison and we Campbells of Leathan have no stronghold to call our own. Many of our friends who lived within the castle walls had no choice but to scatter."

They all fell silent while Logan struggled to contain his fury, for Isla's outspokenness had roused every burning nerve of outrage in his body. It was why he shouldn't be thinking of Mairi's rose-scented allure when he needed to leave here and pursue his brother, who was on his way to Leathan Castle at this very moment. To deliver that Jacobite traitor's daughter with a pardon from the King to save his life!

Fitzroy Campbell did not deserve to be spared.

Logan dropped his spoon into his bowl and cupped his forehead in a hand. "This bloody war," he said.

A hush fell over the table, followed by the small sound of a sniffle.

They all looked up to discover tears streaming down Hamish's cheeks.

"Why is everyone angry?" the boy asked. Then he looked down at his lap. "I think I had an accident."

Isla quickly slid her chair back and took hold of his hand. "Not to worry Hamish. Stand up now. Good gracious, we should know better than to discuss politics at breakfast. Let's go down to the creek and get you cleaned up."

Isla quickly wiped Hamish's chair with a wet cloth, then walked out of the cottage with him. The house grew suddenly quiet, with the exception of the fire crackling in the hearth.

Logan sat back and regarded Mairi across the table. "My apologies."

"No, *I* must apologize," she replied. "My mother has passionate opinions when it comes to clan politics."

Logan adjusted his sling where it was tied at his shoulder. "But I agree with everything she said. I've heard the rumors about the former chief's murder, and I have no respect for the new Campbell chief. He has led the clan to ruin."

Appearing distracted, Mairi gazed out the window. "Sometimes I wish we lived in a different sort of world."

"Aye," he replied, feeling drawn to the serenity in her voice and the faraway look in her eyes. Then she turned those compelling brown eyes to meet his.

"Sometimes I worry about Hamish and the future. He's very sensitive, as you can see. It's probably my fault. I dote on him and encourage him to be ever so careful all the time. I want to keep him safe, yet I feel I am doing him a disservice in a world such as this, because I also want him to be strong…to be able to protect himself."

Logan wet his lips and spoke in a quiet voice. "May I ask what happened to his father?"

Mairi's expression darkened. "It's not a happy story, I'm afraid."

"Please," he said. "I would like to know."

For a long moment she hesitated, as if she weren't sure if she should confide in him. Then she rose from the table and began to clear away the porridge bowls. When at last she began to speak, Logan was first relieved and then instantly riveted.

"His father was an English officer," Mairi said, surprising Logan to no end. "He passed through here one summer afternoon when I was alone in the field gathering up hay for the horses. He claimed to be lost and asked for directions. He was very friendly and helpful. He even helped me load the hay into the wagon. But I made the mistake of falling for his charms. He seemed like such a gentleman at first. Then he took liberties he had no right to take."

She turned away from Logan and carried the bowls to a bucket on the floor in front of the hearth.

"He sounds like no gentleman at all," Logan said with an angry frown while his blood started to boil.

Mairi stood with her back to him, staring into the flames. "I haven't even told you the worst of it." She paused, as if considering whether or not she should continue. Then at last she faced him.

"When I returned to the house in tears with my dress torn, my father realized what had happened. He saddled his horse and went after my attacker." She gazed forlornly out the window. "He rode into the forest and never came back."

Logan's head drew back in confusion. "What happened to him? Did you ever find out?"

"Oh, yes," she replied. "Our friends and neighbors searched for hours. They found him in the woods, dead. He had been shot in the chest. They say he must have drawn his sword, for it was on the ground beside him. I suspect he intended to fight Captain Kearney, but Kearney drew his pistol instead."

"You know his name?" Logan asked. "The officer who killed your father?"

"Aye," she replied. "It was Captain Joseph Kearney and we reported him. Nothing happened, of course. I was accused of being a whore and a temptress. My father's death was deemed self-defense and we were warned never to speak of it again. I didn't, because I didn't want any more harm to come to us. But inside..." She put her fist to her heart. "I was grieving for my father and so deeply enraged, I felt murderous every day."

She returned to the table and cleared away the spoons and milk jug.

"I don't blame you," Logan said. "I'm sorry that happened to you, Mairi."

"So am I. Yet Hamish is a blessing, and for him I am grateful."

Logan bowed his head and nodded. "Of course."

Though he could not disagree with her, he found himself clenching his fist under the table, laboring to hide the fiery rage he felt at the thought of any man mistreating her in such a way. He took a deep breath, counted to ten, and managed to lift his gaze.

"It seems we have something in common," he said. "My father was killed as well, a few years back."

Her eyebrows pulled together in a frown. "I'm sorry. What were the circumstances?"

Knowing he could not tell her everything, Logan shifted in his chair, stalling while he considered how to word it. "A fellow Highlander wanted what he had. He killed him for it."

A knot formed in Logan's gut, for if he had returned home to Leathan Castle sooner, perhaps none of that would have happened.

Mairi slowly circled around the table and laid a comforting hand on his shoulder. Her touch caused his body to come alive with intense longing and a need to confide in her about everything he had kept secret for all these years. The shame, and truth about who he really was.

But he knew he mustn't let that out. If he opened the floodgate, Lord knew what would become of him and Darach.

Mairi's voice was husky and calming. "I wish we could have the things we want without any of the heartbreak and ugliness, but that is life, isn't it? It delivers the good with the bad, and there is nothing we can do to change the past. We must simply accept it, be grateful for the present, and move forward as best we can."

Feeling a deep, almost transcendent fascination, Logan glanced up at her. "That's what my brother always says to me," he replied. "Darach tries to get me to lay the past to rest, when all I want to do is charge ahead at a full gallop and seek justice for things that happened in the past—like my father's murder."

"By justice, do you mean revenge?" she asked pointedly.

Logan considered that for a moment. "I suppose...Aye, that's what I want."

Mairi returned to the other side of the table to pour each of them a second cup of coffee. "I understand that feeling, because I felt that way myself for a long time after that horrific day in the field. I wanted to find Joseph Kearney and drive a dull, rusty blade through his heart...or do worse things to cause him terrible, unthinkable pain. Sometimes I would lie awake at night and dream about all sorts of gruesome acts of violence. Those were the darkest days of my life."

"What changed you?" Logan asked, eager to know her response.

Mairi set the coffeepot down on the stone hearth and took a seat across from him at the table. Picking up her own cup, she sipped it slowly.

"Hamish, of course. When he was born and I first held him in my arms, I looked into his darling face and felt something truly extraordinary. I saw goodness and innocence, and I loved him deeply and exquisitely from the very first moment. I never knew a love like that could even exist. It filled me with lightness and joy. After that discovery, I didn't want to infect him with my hateful thoughts and feelings. I wanted every day to be full of sunshine and happiness for him."

She set down her cup and ran the pad of her forefinger over a deep groove in the wooden table. Logan could only sit there, immersed in suspense, waiting for whatever she might say next.

"Perhaps that's an unrealistic desire," she said at last, "but it was as if I were cleansed by my love for him." She stopped and shook her head at herself. "That must sound silly to you. I cannot believe I just said all that. I'm sure you must think me a dreamer to imagine that life could be pure happiness all the time. It's not possible. I know it's not. That's why I struggle with raising Hamish. I don't want him to grow up without some knowledge of the world and its cruelties." She shook her head regretfully. "But heaven help him. He has no father. He's being raised by two doting females who adore him more than anything in the world. What will become of him later on?"

"I could teach him a few things if you like," Logan offered, hardly realizing the ramifications of what he was saying. He had given no thought whatsoever to the fact that he had to leave here as soon as possible and find his brother. "Like how to hold a sword."

Mairi's cheeks flushed bright red. "Now I am mortified. Honestly, it wasn't my intention to ask anything of you. And I'm not even sure that's what—"

"You didn't ask," he said, interrupting her. "I offered. That is all. It's the least I can do after what you did for me last night."

She stared at him intently for a moment. Then something in her eyes turned cold. She set down her cup and sat back in her chair. "There I go again. Trusting a helpful stranger."

He realized at once what she was referring to. "Do not do that to yourself, Mairi. You've done nothing wrong. You *can* trust me. I have no wish to harm you. Besides, I have only one good arm. All it would take from you is a quick strike to the bad one, and I'd be flat on my back, weeping like a wee bairn. Then you could dump that hot pot of porridge in my face and I'd be utterly defeated and demoralized."

Almost immediately, her mouth curled into a grin and her eyes warmed with laughter. She sat forward slightly and chuckled into her fist. "That is quite an image, Logan. More than I asked for. Although I do not wish to see you demoralized." She lowered her fist and relaxed her hand on the table. "But you are right. I must learn not to be so suspicious of everyone. It has been a challenge for me over the past five years, as you can well imagine. I've not made many new friends."

"It's understandable," he softly said, feeling lost in the depths of her eyes, as if he could forget everything from his own life and simply drift into the misty domain of her soul.

Good God. He was not normally susceptible to such open talk of *feelings.* He'd always been a vigorous, formidable sort. He enjoyed a physical challenge. That's what occupied him most of the time—the use of his body, his muscles, his hands, and thinking about past wrongs. This was new territory. He didn't know what to make of it.

And he'd never felt so completely infatuated.

The door opened just then and Hamish ran straight through the kitchen to the back bedroom, where he disappeared behind the curtain.

Isla entered behind him. "He's embarrassed," she whispered.

Mairi sighed. "I knew it. Poor thing."

Logan slid his chair back and stood. "May I speak with him? Man to man?"

Mairi exchanged an uncertain look with her mother.

"That would be kind of you, Logan," Isla answered for her. "I believe that's why he's so upset. Because it happened in front of *you.*"

Logan nodded with understanding and ventured into the back bedchamber.

>⟩⟨≪

"Hello, Hamish," Logan said, regarding the boy who lay on the bed curled up in a ball, facing the wall. "I have a story I'd like to tell you. Would you like to hear it?"

Hamish sat up and hugged his knees to his chest. His face was beet red, his lips tight with anger. "What kind of story? A real one or a false one? Because sometimes my ma tells me stories about fairies on the moor and I don't like them very much."

"So you want a *true* story, then." Logan approached the bed and sat down at the foot of it.

"Aye. Something with a battle. A really big battle."

Logan glanced up at the ceiling and tapped his finger on his chin. "Hmm, let me see…Aye…I know a good story like that. It's about two young boys. Brothers, actually. This happened a long time ago, before you were born, when many of the clans of Scotland banded together to fight for their freedom on the Battlefield of Sheriffmuir."

"What happened?" Hamish asked.

"Well…The older brother was permitted to go, but his younger brother was only eleven and was forced to stay behind with the women. But he wasn't happy about that, because he wanted more than anything to be a great warrior."

Hamish's eyes grew wide as he hugged his knees closer to his chest. "I want that, too."

"What do you think the boy did?" Logan asked.

"He snuck away and followed."

Logan nodded. "Aye, that's right. He hid inside a barrel and stayed hidden until just before the battle began. Then he found his brother and joined him on the field."

"Was the brother happy to see him?"

"Not at all," Logan replied. "He was always very protective of his younger brother. He told him what terrible things were about to happen, and how many men would die. That's when the boy grew frightened and wished he'd never followed. When the English drums began to beat with a constant *rat-a-tat-tat* on the other side of the field, and the cannons started firing, loud as thunder, the boy was so afraid, he started to cry."

"What did his brother do?"

"His brother didn't see him cry because the boy worked very hard to hide it. He pretended that he wanted to fight."

"What happened?" Hamish asked. "Did the brothers go into battle? Did they live?"

Logan said nothing for a long moment. Then he did what he was so very good at doing. He lied.

"Aye, they were very brave that day and grew up to be great warriors, always fighting at each other's sides."

Hamish smiled and leaned back against the pillow. "That's a good story."

Logan wagged a finger at him. "Aye, but there's a lesson in it."

"What's the lesson?"

"That courage is not the absence of fear, Hamish. Even the bravest of men are afraid sometimes."

Hamish tilted his head to the side. "Are *you* ever afraid?"

"Of course. Last night I had to fix my broken arm, and I knew it was going to hurt. My heart pounded like a hammer and I fainted."

"You *did*?"

"Aye. It was your mother who came to my rescue," Logan continued. "She's a *very* brave woman."

Hamish frowned again. "But she treats me like a baby."

Logan playfully messed the boy's hair. "Give her time, lad. Every day you'll grow bigger. Eventually she'll give you more freedom, and with that comes responsibility. But it's her job to take care of you while you're young. She loves you very much. So mind what she says. Always."

"All right," the boy grudgingly replied.

Logan stood. "Now I have a question for you. Do you know how to swing a sword?"

"Aye!" Hamish scrambled off the bed. "I practice with sticks all the time!"

"How would you like a lesson about how to do it like a *real* warrior?" Logan asked.

Hamish's expression lit up with excitement and he ran out of the room shouting, "Ma! Logan's going to teach me how to fight!"

Logan followed him out to the kitchen where Mairi was standing at the table, wiping the dishes clean. At first he wasn't sure how she would respond, for he did not wish to overstep his bounds, but then a smile spread across her lips and she mouthed the words at him: "*Thank you.*"

He mouthed a private reply: "*You're welcome,*" and being careful with his arm, he left the house to find a couple of suitable sticks for Hamish's first lesson.

⚜

While Mairi completed her morning chores, she watched Logan and Hamish out the window, where they seemed oblivious to the wind gusting around them and the clouds that were rolling in.

First, Logan instructed Hamish about the proper way to hold a sword and how to position his feet. As the hour went on, he showed him some basic maneuvers and practiced them repeatedly.

Soon, it became obvious that Logan was not in optimal condition for such exercises, for he was favoring his broken arm while he held his stick-sword awkwardly with his left, and took frequent breaks.

Hamish, on the other hand, was at his best, listening closely and politely to all of Logan's instructions, and working with great focus to apply what he was learning. They were basic skills, appropriate for a five-year-old, and Mairi found herself distracted from what she was doing. She would stop often to peer out the window, listen, and watch.

Those moments were almost trancelike. Then a surge of excitement would rise up within her at the sight of her son enjoying himself with such fervor. She had to shake herself out of her reverie and force herself to get back to work—only to find herself back at the window a few seconds later.

Perhaps what was so striking was the fact that she never imagined she would ever look at a man again with anything close to desire, but she could not deny the spark of attraction she'd felt at breakfast when Logan listened to her tale of woe, or as she watched him in the back field, swinging a stick-sword. For what could be more appealing than a courageous Scotsman who treated her son with kindness, taught him manly things, and filled him with delight?

Of course, it didn't hurt that Logan was ruggedly handsome and virile. His broad shoulders and thick chest were powerfully sculpted, his movements strong and agile. Normally, she was uneasy around such obvious brawn—for she did not wish to be overpowered ever again—but something about Logan MacDonald eased her concerns and made her feel safe.

A shiver ran up her spine at such a thought, for that had been her undoing five years ago when Joseph Kearney asked for a kiss.

Just one innocent kiss, Mairi. No one has to know...

A sickening knot of anxiety entered her belly as she recalled the sound of his voice. He, too, had made her feel safe and protected, but it had all been a ruse. All he wanted was to trick her and use her for his own selfish, carnal pleasures.

Mairi looked down at the iron pot on the table and scrubbed harder and faster, working vigorously to purge the memories from her head. She hadn't thought of the details of that day in a very long time, but describing parts of it to Logan over breakfast had brought it all back. Given her a reason to think of it.

Her stomach muscles clenched tight, and she scrubbed faster, still.

"Be careful. You're going to kill it," her mother said as she walked into the house carrying a bucket of water.

Mairi looked up and blew a puff of air from her mouth to drive the fallen lock of hair away from her eyes. She stopped scrubbing and leaned back. "And what did this poor innocent pot ever do to me?"

Her mother gave her a knowing look. "Get your head out of the past. Logan MacDonald is a decent man. I can tell."

"You only think that because he agrees with you about politics at Leathan Castle," she replied, returning to her task, more gently this time.

"It's not just that," Isla replied. "He's a fetching young Scot. As strapping as they come. You cannot deny it."

"And you should not be saying such things about a man half your age."

Isla grinned as she set the heavy bucket on the table. "You're right. I have my sights set on another man of a more suitable age. But *you*…"

Mairi carried the iron stew pot to the hearth and set it down. "I don't need to set my sights on anyone, Mother. I am perfectly fine on my own."

"Aye, you're fine," Isla replied. "But life's too short to settle for just fine." She moved to the back window and looked out. "Ah, look at Hamish. I've never seen him so eager to learn."

"Of course he's eager. He's a wee lad without a father, and an impressive warrior from Kinloch Castle is teaching him how to fight."

"Impressive is an understatement," Isla replied as she rose up on her tiptoes to watch Logan from the window. "Just look at those legs."

Mairi slapped her mother on the arm and told her to get back to work.

❧❀❧

Later, when Hamish came inside asking for something to eat, Mairi noticed that Logan did not return with him. She looked out the window and saw him enter the stable and close the door behind him.

He is either leaving us now, or he is in terrible pain.

"Mind your grandmother," she said to her son. "I must go and see to our guest." Reaching for the basket, she discreetly placed the whisky bottle and goblet inside it and left the house.

As she crossed the yard, she felt a rush of disappointment at the notion Logan might be preparing to leave. She quickened her pace, for she didn't want him to set off just yet. First of all, he was in no condition to ride, and secondly, she wanted to thank him for what he'd done for Hamish.

Of course, if she were honest with herself, she would admit there was a third, more significant reason: She wanted to spend a little more time with him—which was a *shocking* realization, for she did not warm to many men.

But how surprisingly refreshing it was to have a man around, despite her usual reservations about strangers, which perhaps said something about Logan's character.

Or perhaps she was simply smitten by his good looks.

Of course, it didn't hurt that he had a broken arm—which made him no physical threat to her, or any of them.

Either way, she wanted to learn more about him and perhaps help him heal.

Lifting the latch on the stable door, she pulled it open on creaking hinges and entered the dim interior. Logan's horse was still in the stall. It was quiet inside. "Logan?"

"Aye."

His response came from the cot in the corner stall, so she ventured closer and found him lying on his back with a knee raised, his eyes closed, his good arm slung across his forehead.

"Are you in pain?" she asked.

"Aye."

She set the basket down and reached into it. "I brought what was left of the whisky."

That got his attention. He uncovered his eyes and slowly sat up. "Thank you, Mairi." While she poured, he said, "I'm cursing my brother right now."

Mairi passed him the glass, then went to fetch the milking stool, set it down on the floor in front of him, and sat down upon it. "I understand that you wish to leave and catch up with him," she said, "but he won't get far today because it's most certainly going to rain. And you're in no condition to ride. You should stay another day."

Logan's eyes lifted. "I can't."

She let out a breath. "It would be a fool's errand anyway, to go after your brother. If you caught up with him today, let me guess…you'd want to thrash him senseless, but there's no question you'll end up the loser in that fight. He'd probably break your *other* arm."

Logan considered that. "I suspect you're right."

Not quite realizing what she was doing, she laid a hand on his knee. "Logan, you cannot ride. You know it as well as I do."

He glanced at her hand on his knee. She quickly withdrew it.

"I don't want to impose," he said.

"You wouldn't be. Hamish would love it if you stayed." She studied his face unhurriedly—his eyes, his cheeks, his lips. "I would like it, too."

One of Logan's eyebrow lifted skeptically. "Really."

"Yes, and I truly mean it," she replied, feeling both foolish and excited at the same time. "So there we have it. You must wait until you are well enough to travel and do some *real* damage."

He inclined his head at her, looking somewhat intrigued, perhaps a little amused.

"I am joking of course," Mairi said. "When you meet up with your brother again, you must talk about what happened and let bygones be bygones."

Logan sipped his whisky. "Easy for you to say."

She tucked a stray tendril of hair behind her ear and felt a pleasant tingling in the pit of her belly at the notion of having Logan stay another night.

"Well, then," she said, rising to her feet and setting the milking stool back against the wall. "Get some rest this morning, and later I'll bring you some lunch."

Picking up the whisky bottle, Logan refilled his cup, which he had placed on the ground at his feet. "With any luck I'll be stewed to the gills by then."

She chuckled softly. "Just don't come into the kitchen singing and dancing. I'll have a hard time explaining that to Hamish."

He met her gaze, reached for her hand and squeezed it. "Thank you, Mairi. You're a good woman."

The warmth of his touch sent an explosion of fire into her blood, which nearly caused her to lose her breath. But it was not fear or panic she felt—which was usually the case whenever a man touched her for any reason.

This morning, there was an unmistakable pooling of desire in her belly. A dangerous heat in her core. For a moment she hungered for more.

Logan held on to her fingers for a few seconds. Gently, he stroked her knuckles with the pad of his thumb.

"You're not in the habit of welcoming a man's touch," he said plainly.

"Nay, I am not."

"It's understandable, but there's nothing to fear from me, Mairi. I only want to say thank you. That's all."

She should have said something like "You're welcome" or "It's been no trouble at all." Instead, she slid her hand from his, backed away and hurried out of the stable, leaving the door wide open behind her.

As she hastened across the windy yard to the cottage, she felt a few raindrops strike her cheeks and forehead. She shivered from the unseasonable chill from the north. The shock of it woke her to her embarrassment for simply walking out without saying another word to him.

"You foolish woman," she said to herself. "He's going to think you are daft."

Meanwhile, as Logan stood in the open doorway of the stable, watching Mairi dash into the cottage, his thoughts were heading in another direction entirely, for his body was alive with yearnings to touch her again, to hold her in his arms, to breathe in her delectable womanly scent and press his mouth urgently to hers.

Easy now, Logan said to himself as he turned and walked back to his cot. *She's not the sort of woman you can trifle with.*

And he really needed to be on his way.

CHAPTER

FIVE

❧

"We can't just leave him out there," Isla said as she spooned hot broth into a cup. "The rain has been coming down in buckets all day and the chill has gone straight to my bones. The poor man must be shivering under his tartan. Imagine the discomfort, with that broken arm…"

Mairi moved to the front window and looked out. "You're right. It's a beast of a day. We should bring him inside by the fire."

"Finally, you're making sense. And later, when it gets dark, he can sleep in your bed."

Mairi whirled around to face Isla. "I beg your pardon?"

Isla rolled her eyes and laughed. "Not *together* with you. It's going to be a cold, wet night, lass. You'll give him your bed and sleep with us."

Mairi faced the window again. "*Mmm.* Maybe you're right. We should bring him in." She considered sending Hamish out to extend the invitation, but the rain was coming down hard and she wasn't sure how much of the whisky Logan might have consumed. Hamish would be soaked and Logan could be completely inebriated. "I'll go and fetch him." She reached for her shawl and raised it over her head.

Seconds later, she was at the stable door, flinging it open and darting inside.

"Gracious," she whispered, lowering her shawl and shaking out the rain, while the wind pummeled the stable from all directions.

The chickens clucked and fluttered about, and Logan's horse stomped around skittishly.

"Relax everyone," she whispered. "It's only a rainstorm."

Tiptoeing to the back stall, she found Logan resting soundly on his side, facing the wall. Not yet ready to wake him, she allowed her eyes a moment to roam the full length of his body, from his broad shoulders beneath the loose white shirt, to his narrow hips and those long, muscular legs.

You shouldn't be doing this, Mairi. You should not be looking at him like that…

Leisurely, he rolled over and gazed up at her. "Can I help you, lass?"

Taking a step back—and feeling as if she'd been caught like a thief in the night, stealing naughty glances—she spoke casually. "I only came to see if you wished to join us inside by the fire. It's a miserable day, and it's only going to get worse."

He slowly sat up. "That's very kind of you, Mairi. If you're certain I would not be intruding…."

"Not at all. We couldn't possibly enjoy our supper with you out here in the cold. Please, come with me." She held out a hand.

His green eyes glimmered with appreciation as he accepted it and rose to his feet, looking tall, capable and brawny, even with his arm bound to his ribs in the sling. He stood for a moment, gazing down at her while the rain struck the window pane.

Her heart thudded in her chest. "Did you finish the whisky?" she asked, feeling like she could use a wee dram herself, just to calm her nerves.

"Not all of it."

She looked down and spotted it on the floor next to the bed. "I'll bring it inside then."

She bent to pick it up and placed it in the basket with the goblet, knowing the entire time that it was merely a reason to turn away from him before he recognized how flustered she was feeling.

And how strangely, unexpectedly exhilarated she was by that.

⚜

The cold rain fell mercilessly for the rest of the day and long into the night, while the wind howled up and down the glen.

"I owe you another debt," Logan said to Mairi after Isla took Hamish to bed—in a blatantly obvious attempt to leave them alone together. "I would have been in no condition to brave this storm on the road with my arm in a sling. Thank you for convincing me to stay on another day."

Mairi sat in a chair across from him, in front of the warm, crackling fire, sipping her wine. "There is no debt to repay, Logan," she replied. "Your company this evening was more than enough to satisfy us all. Hamish greatly enjoyed your stories of adventure as a scout." She leaned forward and spoke conspiratorially. "But tell me the truth now. Were they all true?"

He leaned forward as well until their faces were very close. She could almost feel the beat of his breath on her lips. "I might have exaggerated a detail or two, just a wee bit."

She found herself smiling and beguiled by his candor, the sculpted contours of his face, and the glimmer of mischief in his eyes.

Mairi sat back. "Your secret is safe with me."

He leaned back also and, in the flickering light, regarded her with interest.

Perhaps it was the wine, but she felt unusually adventurous herself—and wickedly flirtatious—which was not like her at all. Or perhaps it was simply the passage of time and the fading of certain unpleasant memories from her mind.

Or perhaps it was the man himself.....

For the next two hours, they sat and talked openly about every possible subject under the sun—Scottish politics and farming, stories from their respective childhoods. He spoke affectionately about his over-protective brother, and she told him about her father and the brothers she'd loved but lost at the Battle of Sheriffmuir.

Soon she couldn't keep from yawning, and Logan set down his glass. "I'm keeping you up."

"Not at all," she replied, not wanting him to think she was disinterested in his company. "I haven't enjoyed myself like this in a long time. Not since…Oh, I can't even remember when."

He spoke softly, "I feel the same way, Mairi. Right now, I'm almost *glad* my brother broke my arm."

Her eyebrows lifted in surprise, but before she could comment on that, the sound of approaching hooves and men's voices outside in the yard caused her heart to explode with panic. Her eyes darted to the door.

"Are you expecting anyone tonight?" Logan asked.

"In this foul weather? No."

He rose from his chair. "Where's your pistol?"

She rose also and bent to fetch it from the box under the storage cabinet.

"It's here."

"Give it to me, lass."

She handed it to him without the slightest hesitation.

"Do you have any other weapons in the house?" he asked. "A sword or a dirk I might use?"

"My father's sword. It's in my bedchamber, on top of the wardrobe." By now, her belly was on fire with terror, for it sounded as if there were a number of men outside, not just one or two. It was like something out of one of her nightmares.

Logan moved swiftly toward the curtain that led to her mother's room where Mairi's son lay sleeping, checked on them, then crossed to her room on the other side of the kitchen. "I'll wait in here. Answer the door and see what they want. Maybe they're just looking for shelter. If that's the case, send them to the stable. Tell them your son is ill with a fever and no one should enter."

Nodding her head quickly, she lifted the bottom of her skirt and unsheathed the small blade she always kept hidden in her boot. When she lowered the hem, she noticed Logan watching her from the door to her room. She merely shrugged, and he gave her look of approval, as if he understood exactly why she carried it.

In that moment, a knock rapped urgently at the door.

Mairi glanced over her shoulder to wait until Logan was hidden behind the curtain, then she opened the door a small crack.

A tall, flaxen-haired English soldier in a rain-sodden cloak stood outside in the furious downpour. "I beg your pardon, madam," he said, grimacing with discomfort in the cold. "Would you allow us to take shelter in your stable for the night?"

The sound of his voice—that familiar, well-bred English accent—sent a shiver of revulsion down her spine.

Mairi studied his eyes, searching for signs of deceitfulness or drunkenness. All she saw was a man shivering in the cold, appearing rather desperate.

"How many are with you?" she asked, leaning to peer over his shoulder.

"Five in all," he replied. "I apologize for the inconvenience, but we will require nothing more than the use of your stable. Perhaps a few eggs in the morning if you can spare them."

Though it was pitch dark outside and the rain was coming down in a merciless fury from the clouds, Mairi was able to make out the shadowy figures of four men on horseback, braving the storm in their saddles.

"Aye, you may take shelter here," she replied, "and help yourselves to some eggs in the morning. But please be gone at first light."

He bowed and fingered the brim of his hat. "Much obliged, madam."

He shouted orders to his men, while Mairi quickly shut the door and locked it.

Exhaling with relief, she turned around and tipped her head back against the door. Logan emerged from behind the curtain with her father's sword in hand.

"Did you hear that?" she asked.

"Aye. You did well, lass. Now go get in bed with your mother and son. I'll stay awake and keep watch."

She blinked a few times, feeling rather dizzy as her rapid, out-of-control pulse finally began to slow to a normal pace. "Logan, what would you have done if they tried to come inside?"

"If they intended to do you harm, lass, I would have killed them."

She felt her forehead crinkle with disbelief—and fascination. "Even with your broken arm? You believe you could have done that?"

"Aye." He strode closer and set the sword on the table. "Never underestimate the element of surprise."

Her body rhythms began to slow as he grew nearer with every step. By the time he reached her, she felt completely spellbound, and ever so grateful for his presence.

Logan stood before her, his golden hair falling forward around his face. He smelled of leather and wood smoke, and she wanted to reach out and touch him—to lay her hands on his solid chest, to step into his arms and feel safe there.

"Do you often get Redcoats knocking at your door?" he asked.

"Nay," she replied. "But I suspect it might become a regularity, now that the Campbell stronghold has fallen to the English."

Logan's eyes roamed over her face, then he reached out, as if he were about to lay his hand upon her cheek.

Instinct took over. Mairi turned her face away. "Please, don't."

With his hand still hovering in mid-air, Logan tilted his head to the side. "I only wanted to tuck that stray tendril behind your ear," he explained.

Her heart raced as she met his gaze again. "I'm sorry. I didn't mean to react like that."

"No need to apologize." He lowered his hand to his side. "You should get some rest now. I'll keep an eye on things."

"Thank you," she replied shakily, wondering why she'd turned away from him when only seconds before, she'd wanted to lay her hands on his chest, feel safe in his arms. Perhaps even feel his lips upon hers and stoke the fires of desire that were growing inside her.

She'd never believed her body would ever know such feelings again, and yet despite desire, she had recoiled from his touch. What was wrong with her?

"Good night, lass," Logan said, his gaze deep and penetrating, urging her to go.

"Good night," she replied in a whisper, not wanting to leave him, but feeling confused and knowing that it would be best.

⚔

The following morning, Mairi woke to the faint sound of voices in the yard. Sitting up in bed beside Hamish and her mother, she listened carefully, alert for a knock at the door or some other such disturbance.

When nothing happened, she slid off the bed, stood and padded to the window to carefully look out. The morning sun—just beginning its rise—revealed five Redcoats in her yard, mounting their horses and discussing in which direction they should travel. There was some disagreement until the ranking officer laid out a plan.

A moment later, they were gone, by way of the swollen creek, and then they entered the forest.

Her mother sat up. "Have they left?"

"Aye," Mairi replied, moving to the bed to kiss Hamish on the forehead. "Sleep late if you wish," she whispered. "I'll take care of breakfast."

As she swept the curtain aside, she found Logan in the kitchen, just turning away from the window with the pistol in his hand, her father's sword sheathed in his weapon belt. He lowered the pistol and released the hammer.

"Were you up all night?" she asked.

"Aye, though I might have dozed off once or twice."

She approached him. "You must be exhausted. Why don't you get some sleep? Please take my bed. It will be awhile before breakfast is ready."

He agreed and handed the pistol to her.

"I can't thank you enough," she said.

"No thanks are necessary," he replied, as he moved to disappear behind the curtain to her room, leaving her feeling very regretful for her behavior the night before.

⊰≋⊱

After returning to bed after breakfast, Logan slept a good part of the day and woke to the delicious aroma of meat stew. In that moment, he experienced a minor epiphany and decided to make no mention of hurrying off to pursue his brother while he contemplated it.

For one thing, the hour was growing late, but more importantly, he couldn't fathom the idea of mounting his horse and saying good-bye to Mairi Campbell. The incident with the Redcoats the night before had been disconcerting to say the least, and he wanted to make sure they did not return.

Or perhaps he simply wanted to remain in Mairi's presence a little longer and assure himself that she was not torturing herself over what had passed between them the night before—when he'd tried to touch her.

There might have been a hint of a challenge in there somewhere...for after seeing her flinch, he wanted more than anything to prove he could be trusted, that he had no wish to harm her. He wanted her to know—and truly believe—that a man's touch wasn't always to be feared.

It was not an entirely selfless ambition. It was, in fact, quite the opposite. She was the most stunningly beautiful woman he had ever laid eyes upon, and not only that, she was strong, brave and resilient, and full of goodness—for she had somehow managed to put hatred and vengeance aside for the sake of love for her son.

How was such a thing possible? How had she done it?

Logan had sat up all night, keeping watch over this household and pondering the magnitude of those questions. When he woke to the smell of meat stew, he was in absolute awe of Mairi Campbell. It was as if the night sky had exploded with stars before his eyes. If she had found peace in her heart, after all she'd been through, maybe it was possible for him, too.

But with that epiphany came uncomfortable questions about his own integrity. *Could* he really be trusted? Mairi didn't know the first thing about him. He was not who he claimed to be. He was lying to her with every look, every word, every smile.

It had never bothered him to tell a lie before—his whole life had been a lie—but on that particular evening, his gut had a knot in it the size of a boulder.

⋘⊰⊱⋙

Logan enjoyed three helpings of Mairi's succulent meat stew, and after supper, they again sat together in front of the fire after Isla took Hamish to bed.

They talked of her neighbors and how her father had come to reside on this land, and how he had met her mother when they were very young.

Logan shared more stories from his life as a scout, and through it all, neither of them mentioned the awkward moment from the night before when she had recoiled from his touch.

It was long past midnight when they finally said good-night. Logan returned to his cot in the stable to allow Mairi a good night's sleep in her own bed.

For hours, he lay awake, replaying their conversations over and over in his mind and imagining in splendid, vivid detail what would happen if he touched her again…and she did *not* recoil.

⋘⊰⊱⋙

"I'm glad you decided to stay another day," Mairi said the next morning, startling Logan from his crouched position at the edge of the creek where he was awkwardly attempting to shave his stubbly beard with one hand.

Isla had been kind enough to loan him her late husband's blade and shaving brush, as well as a bar of soap, but he was having a devil of a time managing everything. He felt like he had the skills of a three-year-old.

He tried to stand and greet Mairi, but with one arm still in a sling, and the other hand fumbling with the soap dish and blade, he lost his balance and fell backwards onto his haunches on the grass. His arm throbbed with pain.

"Oh dear," Mairi said, hurrying forward to help him. "That was my fault. I shouldn't have snuck up on you like that."

Logan winced and tried again to get up. "It's all right, lass. It does a man good to be reminded that he shouldn't take anything for granted. This makes me appreciate both my hands all the more."

She hooked her arm under his and helped him to rise, then pointed a finger at the lather on his chin. "You missed a few spots. Right there. Would you like some help?"

Suddenly his infirmity felt less like a curse and more like a blessing, if it meant he could spend some time close and alone with her. He decided to play it up. "I *was* having some trouble. Would you mind?" He held out the blade.

Mairi smiled and took it from his open hand. "Not at all. This was something I used to do for my father, though it was a long time before he allowed me to hold the blade. I must have been at least twelve."

"Who could blame him?" Logan replied. "An unsteady hand could inadvertently cut a man's throat and end his life—which would result in a lifetime of guilt for the offender. No father would wish to inflict that upon his child."

Mairi nodded, a twinkle in her eye. "Aye, he was probably wise to wait. Shall we sit down?"

Logan followed her lead and sat on the grass with his legs stretched out before him, crossed at the ankles, while the creek—swollen from the recent rains—rushed fast and thunderously over the rocks beside them.

Mairi crouched on her knees. "Hamish has been hounding me to ask if you'll give him another fighting lesson," she said as she swirled the brush around in the cup of water. "I'm not sure what to tell him. I don't wish to presume anything and I know what it cost you last time. The pain to your arm."

Logan tipped his head back to allow her better access to his jaw and throat. "I'd be happy to give him another lesson. I feel stronger today. I'm well-rested and my arm is not smarting so much."

Mairi applied soap to the brush and lathered his chin and jawline. "I'd like to keep it that way." She gave him a cautioning look. "No sense testing your luck."

"I couldn't agree more."

He closed his eyes at the scraping sound of the blade, while he luxuriated in the knowledge that it was Mairi who held it. It was not exactly the same as the touch of her skin, but it was an oddly intimate act she was performing.

"Do you think your brother has reached Leathan Castle by now?" she asked, reminding him of his life away from there and the circumstances that were supposed to be at the forefront of his mind.

"Nay, he won't arrive until tomorrow at the earliest."

"Are you sorry you won't be at his side?"

Leaning back on his good arm and opening his eyes to gaze at Mairi in the sparkling morning light, Logan was sorry about nothing at all. At least not in that moment.

"Surprisingly, no."

She stopped what she was doing and lifted the blade away from his chin.

"Why is that, sir?"

"Because there is something I'm far more interested in, right here."

Mairi sat back on her heels and lowered her thick black lashes as she wiped the soap and stubble from the blade. "After all my threats and warnings on that first night, are you daring to *flirt* with me, Logan MacDonald? While I am holding a blade that could cut your throat?"

"Aye," he replied flatly, lifting his chin higher. "Sometimes a man has to do what a man has to do, no matter the cost."

The corner of Mairi's full cherry lips curled up in a small grin, and her liquid brown eyes lifted. She leaned forward on her knees and touched the blade to his cheek, where she scraped it slowly and firmly across his hard stubble. "You're a brave man."

"And you're a lovely woman. Far too good for the likes of me."

Their eyes remained locked on each other's while the air between them sizzled with heat, and somehow Logan knew that if he touched her then, she would not flinch or pull away.

But *damn*, he shouldn't. That would most definitely be stepping over the line, and what right did he have? He'd be riding off soon and there was no guarantee he'd ever be able to come back….

Mairi swallowed hard and wet her lips.

God…what he *really* wanted to do was tumble her onto her back, crush her body with his, then take her mouth with a scorching, savage kiss that would leave them both breathless and hungry for more.

At least it would leave *him* hungry for more. His passion would probably scar her for life.

Thank God he was a disciplined man. He made no move to touch or kiss her.

"My heart is racing," she said rather breathlessly.

"Mine, too, lass." She had no idea.

Then, to his surprise, Mairi lowered the blade from his cheek, leaned closer and touched her lips to his. It was a mere butterfly of a kiss—soft, light and warm—and it left him dangerously ravenous for more. He wanted to plunge into her with all his might.

That's why his heart was pounding so fast, because he was fighting an inner battle to keep his out-of-control lust at bay.

Just then, a movement from farther down the creek caught Logan's eye.

Bloody hell. Five English soldiers were approaching on horseback—the same five who had spent the rainy night in Mairi's stable. He hadn't heard the hoofbeats on account of the rushing water in the creek.

"Get up, lass."

Logan quickly stood, pushed her behind him, and drew the pistol from his belt. He aimed it at the officer on the lead horse.

The soldiers trotted closer and stopped in front of them. "Put your weapon away, Highlander. We mean you no harm."

"I mean you no harm either," Logan replied, without lowering the gun.

The officer studied him for a moment. "What happened to your arm?"

"I had a disagreement with my brother," Logan replied in a cool voice.

"Your brother! *Hmph.* You Highlanders certainly are a savage bunch." The officer leaned to the side to get a better look at Mairi. "Are you the woman who gave us shelter the other night?"

She stepped out from behind Logan. "Aye."

"Well then, we owe you a debt of thanks." His gaze roamed freely down the length of her body from head to foot. "May I ask your name?"

"It's Mairi Campbell." She lifted her chin defiantly.

"Pretty name. It's a pleasure to meet you, Mairi."

Logan's blood boiled at the openly flirtatious tone in the officer's voice and the crude leering in the other men's eyes.

"I'm her husband," he added, cocking the hammer of the pistol.

The officer held out a gloved hand. "No need to get jumpy, Highlander."

"I'm not jumpy. If I was, you'd know it."

The officer regarded him carefully, as if he were weighing his options and considering what to say or do next.

"Is there something we can do for you?" Logan asked directly, with more than a little impatience.

The officer sat up straighter in the saddle and gazed off toward the mountains. "Nothing this morning. We're just making the rounds. Getting to know the locals. Anyone else live with you in that house?"

"Our son," Mairi replied, "and my mother."

"How old is your son?" the officer asked.

"He's just a wee lad."

The officer turned his eyes to Logan. "You mentioned a brother. Does he live there as well?"

Neither Mairi, nor Logan, offered a response.

"I'll take that as a no." A flash of derision darkened the officer's eyes. "Very well, then. We will be on our way. Pleasant day to you both." He thumbed the brim of his tricorne hat, urged his horse into a trot and rode on, leading the others north along the creek.

Logan waited until they were out of sight before he tucked the pistol into his belt. Then his body alerted to the sensation of Mairi's small hand sliding into his and squeezing it tightly.

He turned to face her and was shocked when she threw her arms around his neck and pressed her cheek to his shoulder at the top of the sling.

"Thank you," she whispered, holding tight. "I didn't want to be, but I was afraid."

Logan could think of only one thing to say. "He wasn't one of them, was he? The man who dishonored you five years ago?"

Mairi shook her head and stepped back. "No. If he was, I probably would have grabbed the pistol from you and shot him in the heart. Not that he ever had one." She dropped her gaze to the grass. "My legs are shaking. My knees have gone weak." She touched the heel of her hand to her forehead.

Logan cupped her elbow to hold her steady. "Sit down, lass."

In one smooth motion, they sank together onto the grass where he pulled her onto his lap. Mairi curled up against him with her cheek on his shoulder, her arms locked around his neck. He felt her hot breath against his collarbone as she nuzzled her nose into the opening of his shirt. It was enough to light a hot fire of lust in his blood, though he knew it was not lust that *she* was feeling. Gratitude was something else entirely.

A few nights ago, when she'd found him in the field, he had been a potential threat to her safety, but today, he knew he had become her friend and protector. They were now on the same side.

Heaven help him, he *liked* it. He *liked* that she was warming to him and beginning to trust, even though she did not know him at all.

Mairi let out a sigh and buried her face even closer to his neck. Logan felt himself grow hard and had to fight rigorously to suppress the workings of his body, for she was sitting on his lap and there could be no hiding his arousal.

To his surprise, she lifted her face, studied his eyes for a few sizzling seconds, then touched her lips to his again—this time more deeply and aggressively.

That was that. Logan could no longer resist. He rocked her forward in his one good arm, while thrusting his tongue into her mouth and relishing the sweet delectable flavor of her soft, warm lips.

She pressed her body closer and slid her hand to the side of his face where she stroked his cheek. Raking her fingers through his hair, she dragged her mouth from his. "I never imagined a kiss could feel so good. I had no idea I could ever know this kind of pleasure."

"It does feel good, lass," he ground out, pausing to admire her beauty in the morning light, willing himself to stop. But he couldn't. He crushed her mouth with his again and cupped the back of her head in his good hand, groaning with need.

The kiss was hot and wet and he felt a painful ache of desire in his groin that begged for release. His hand slid down over Mairi's shoulder, along the top of her arm and finally to her breast, which he cupped in his open palm.

Suddenly, Mairi gasped and pulled her mouth away. She slid off his lap, onto the grass, where she sat back on her heels.

Logan could do nothing but struggle to shake off the arousal and subsequent frustration. He hadn't meant to break the spell of their magical first kiss. He certainly hadn't wanted to frighten her or spoil what should have been a pleasant experience. But as he looked into her startled eyes, he decided the distance now between them was probably for the best. He was *glad* she had put a stop to it.

Wise choice, lass.

Mairi's lips parted and she blinked a few times, as if she were confused by her response and couldn't make sense of it.

"You don't feel safe with me," he said matter-of-factly.

"But I do," she replied, still staring at him intently. "It's not that I don't trust you. It's just that…" She bowed her head and shook it at herself. "I think I'm broken inside."

"Nay, lass you're not broken. You're perfect. I'm the one who's broken, and you should be with a man who is worthy of you. A man who will go slow with you, a man who will take the time to show you how to love him…a man who will never leave you. I cannot promise you that, for I'm in a hurry to leave here as soon as I am able."

"To satisfy your hunger for revenge, you mean," she said. "To avenge your father's death."

"Aye."

She glanced at his arm in the sling, then back up at his weary eyes. "You could choose to let all of that go, and remain here."

He shook his head. "But I do not wish to let it go."

"Why not? Doesn't that constant hatred make you feel angry and unhappy?"

"It does, which is why I must snuff out the thing at which my anger is directed."

She thought about that for a moment. "I do not believe you will be any happier if you do whatever it is you intend to do at Leathan Castle. Isn't that your goal? To take revenge on the man who killed your father? That's what you told me the other night, but it will not bring your father back. It won't change the past."

Logan pinched the bridge of his nose and wanted only to change the subject, for this was far more complicated than she knew.

"I shouldn't have touched you like that," he said. "It won't happen again, lass." He made a move to rise.

"No, please..." Mairi stopped him with the touch of her hand on his knee. "You did nothing wrong, Logan, and I don't want you to go. Please stay one more night. Just one. And I liked it when you held me. Truly I did."

Logan spoke gently. "I liked it, too, lass, but holding you like that will most certainly lead to something else." He got to his feet and held out his hand. "We should be getting back. Hamish will be wondering what became of you."

Mairi gazed up at Logan, hesitating to take his hand.

"What's wrong?" he asked.

"I don't know. I just felt as if I'd lived this moment before. In a dream or something. Do you ever have that feeling?" She placed her hand in his and rose to her feet just as Hamish came running from the house with an empty bucket.

"Ma! Did you see the soldiers?" he shouted.

Mairi stepped back, and Logan again had to suppress his desires, for he'd wanted to kiss her again just then.

"Aye," she replied. "They're just scouting the area. That is all. There's nothing to be afraid of."

"I wasn't afraid!" Hamish said as he reached them. "I liked their uniforms. They're bright red."

Mairi glanced at Logan with concern. "Yes, they are, but I prefer the Campbell tartan. Don't you?"

Hamish looked up at Logan with a tilt of his small head. "Do you prefer tartan?"

"Aye," Logan replied.

"Then I prefer tartan, too." Hamish ran to the creek, filled his bucket, and started back to the house.

"I should finish shaving," Logan said brusquely, needing some time to be alone.

"And I should go back with him." Mairi turned to go, but stopped and faced him. "Will you stay at least one more night? Please?"

Logan's gaze roamed the features of her face and the attractive curve of her hips. He felt another stirring of desire, and for once, he told the truth.

"I cannot imagine leaving here today."

Her smile was radiant as the sun, and it left him feeling shaken and uncertain about everything he'd felt so sure about just a few short days ago.

CHAPTER

SEVEN

That night after supper, Logan thanked Isla and Mairi for the delicious meal, said goodnight to Hamish, and announced that he would be retiring to his own cot in the stable, for he was still unsettled by what had occurred between him and Mairi on the bank of the creek.

He knew he couldn't be around her—not without wanting to entice her into his bed. And that simply could not be. First of all, he wasn't sure he could trust himself to go slow with her, which was what she needed—a man who would not be rough or aggressive.

Besides, she was not some happy-go-lucky tavern wench or a lonely widow looking to satisfy a sensual urge. Mairi was a young mother raising a son on her own—a woman who had been treated appallingly five years ago by a despicable wretch of a man.

Logan was also a wretch of a man, but in a different way, and she deserved better. She needed more than what he could give. So he had to put a stop to this flirtation before he was tempted to go beyond the point of no return.

As a result, before he walked out their door, her turned to Isla and Mairi, thanked them for their hospitality and told them he would be leaving at first light.

Mairi paced about her room, chewing on a thumbnail and wondering frantically if she could throw caution to the wind, sneak out of the house like a wanton woman, and visit Logan in the stable.

It was past midnight, and he intended to leave in the morning, even after he'd assured her that morning that he wished to stay. *What changed his mind?* She almost couldn't bear the thought of saying good-bye and never knowing any further intimacies with him. It was like a kick to the stomach, for she had felt herself opening up physically for the first time in many years, like a flower blooming in the early spring, even while snow still covered parts of the ground.

She wanted to continue that exploration…to see what might be possible. If she were honest with herself, she would admit that she was wildly attracted to Logan, she couldn't take her eyes off him, and she simply *wanted* him, in the physical sense. She was hungry for his touch and for the promise of more pleasures than she had known when he'd kissed her that morning.

Moving to the window, Mairi gazed out at the darkness but saw only her own reflection in the glass. Her dark hair spilled loosely over her shoulders. She had spent far too much time brushing it out earlier, yanking roughly at her locks while trying to talk herself out of caring that Logan had decided to leave.

It doesn't matter. He doesn't want to be here and you don't know what you're asking for. Remember how you panicked and pulled away when he touched you? Why would anything be different if you went to the stable tonight?

Turning away from the window, she slipped into bed and pulled the covers up to her chin. *Go to sleep, Mairi. No good can come of this. He's leaving in the morning. Just let him go.*

But when she tried to close her eyes, her body remembered the sensations by the creek that morning. Logan's soft, warm lips touching hers...the lush pressure of his tongue as it entered her mouth, and how she had delighted in it. A pleasurable ache began between her thighs and she wondered if perhaps this might be her one and only opportunity to learn how to enjoy a man's touch—with someone who actually aroused her passions. It was something she'd believed, just a few days ago, to be an impossibility.

Mairi felt strangely empowered suddenly, for she knew that Logan was wounded—both physically and in other ways. Perhaps this was what she needed, to be with a man who was also broken, inside and out. Perhaps they could be broken together—maybe even help each other to heal.

⚜

Logan stood in the dim lantern light, inside the front stall, running his good hand over the length of Tracker's back after refreshing his bucket of water.

Logan assured himself that he had done the right thing by announcing it was time for him to leave. He couldn't continue to waste precious hours and days convalescing while Darach was making his way to Leathan Castle to deliver the pardon that would save the life of their mortal enemy, Fitzroy Campbell.

At the very least, Logan wanted to stop Darach from reaching the castle in time to stop the execution. *Let the villain hang.* But what he wanted even more was to look the miserable rotter straight in the eye as he gasped his last breath, and tell him that he was dying at the hands of Ronald James Campbell's son— son of the chief he'd murdered in cold blood for the sake of his own ambitions. Logan wanted Fitzroy to understand *exactly* who was sending him to hell. Logan would follow him there himself, if that's what was required.

Just then, a noise outside caused him to turn his attention to the door. It swung open slowly, creaking like the ghostly howl of an old cat. In the moonlight, Mairi tiptoed inside.

His heart leapt.

Wearing nothing but her shift and a blood-red shawl—and with her hair falling in shiny black waves over her shoulders—she closed the door behind her and continued past the stall, evidently unaware of Logan's presence there.

He moved quietly to the wooden rail and watched her creep to the back of the stable and peer down at his empty cot in the shadows.

"Logan?" she whispered, moving closer.

His entire body and soul thrilled at the sight of her, especially when she had no idea he was watching her. There was a playfulness in him suddenly, for he was reminded of a child's game of hide and seek—even though he had prayed earlier that she would not come to him. That she would know better than to sneak in here and take chances with a man who wanted desperately to bed her. Thoroughly and passionately. Just once...

Hah! What the devil was he thinking? Once would never be enough. He was deluding himself.

"Logan?" She moved closer and reached out to the pile of bedclothes in the shadows.

"I'm here," he said at last in a low, husky voice.

Mairi whirled around and laid a hand over her heart. "You frightened me. I didn't see you there."

"I know," he casually replied, moving out of the stall and closing the gate behind him. "I couldn't sleep. But what are *you* doing here, Mairi?"

They met face to face in the center of the stable, beneath the glow of the hanging lantern.

"I couldn't sleep either," she replied. "Not after you said you were leaving. I thought you might stay a little longer."

He shook his head. "I can't. And you know why."

But did she? Did she know the real reason why it was best that he leave here as soon as possible?

"Because you want to find your brother," she answered for him, "and have your revenge."

Logan was very used to lying. It would have been so easy to say yes, that was why he needed to go, but instead, the truth came spilling out faster than he could stop it.

"It's not just that. You remember what happened by the creek this morning. I took liberties that made you uncomfortable. If I stay, it will only happen again."

"Maybe I *want* it to happen," she said.

His head drew back in surprise. "I don't think you know what you're saying, Mairi."

She scoffed at that and spoke in a frantic flood of words. "I know *exactly* what I'm saying, and I came here because I couldn't stop thinking about you tonight…How it felt when you kissed me. I experienced feelings I didn't think I could ever feel again, and it made me believe I could be a normal woman. A woman who enjoys being with a man." She paused and looked down at the hay-strewn floor. "Sometimes I think about Hamish never having any brothers or sisters, and I wish that he could have a normal life, too—"

Alarm bells began to chime inside Logan's head, and he frowned. "Is that what you want from me, Mairi? A brother for Hamish? Is that why you came out here?"

Her eyes lifted and she blinked a few times. "Good heavens, no. That's not what I was trying to say at all. This is coming out all wrong. I just want to believe that it's possible...that there is hope for me—that someday I might be able to give myself to a man. Without reservation."

He shook his head. "It shouldn't be me, Mairi."

She did not back down. She took a step forward and laid her hand on his chest. "Why not?"

He felt a sizzle of energy run through him as he beheld her dazzling beauty in the lamplight—the striking contrast of her dark, midnight hair, to her rosy cheeks, and clear ivory complexion. The attractive curve of her hips beneath the loose, fluttering shift. The scent of roses that inundated his senses and filled him with physical need.

Most of all, the luxuriant, sumptuous breasts—one of which he'd cupped in his hand that very morning.

The memory of it set his impulses on fire and he began to wonder, selfishly, how far she would let him go before she changed her mind.

Would he be able to stop if she asked him to?

"I want to be alone with you tonight," she said in a quiet, seductive voice. "I want you to touch me."

Logan imagined at once all the decadent, licentious ways he could do exactly that. Ways he could help her learn to enjoy a man's touch.

His touch.

An intense surge of desire swelled beneath his kilt.

This was dangerous.

"You shouldn't be here, Mairi," Logan forced himself to say. "You should go back to the house."

"I don't want to. I'm not afraid of what you're thinking about."

"You *should* be," he replied. "And how do you know what I'm thinking about?"

"Because it's the same thing *I'm* thinking about." She drew a line with her finger…down the center of his chest to his stomach, and paused at the top of his kilt.

Logan's body exploded into a flood of painful carnal lust. Lord help him, if Mairi didn't leave now, she was going to find herself on her back in the next few seconds.

"I'm leaving in the morning," he reminded her. "Nothing's going to change that."

"I don't care. All I want is tonight."

"You'll regret it. And you'll hate me in the morning."

Her expression darkened. "No, I won't."

She was far too tenacious. She wasn't heeding his words at all.

"I won't hate you," she said, "because I trust you to be gentle with me. To go slow. That's all I ask. Can you do that? We could start on top of my shift, and wait until I'm ready before you put your hands under it."

He was finding it harder and harder to resist the provocative images she was describing.

"You shouldn't trust a man you know nothing about," he tried to argue.

"But I *do* know you."

"No, you do not, lass," he replied tersely. "You don't know the first thing about me."

She inclined her head at him and narrowed her gaze. "I know enough. I know that you won't hurt me, and that if I change my mind and ask you to stop, you will."

He scoffed. "You have more confidence in me than I do, because I'm burning for you, Mairi. All I want to do right now is drag you to that bed, push you onto it, and take my pleasure inside of you. Thrust into you, deep and hard, over and over, faster and faster. *There, now.* Is that what you want? To be over-powered? I didn't think so." He pointed at the door. "Leave now while you still can."

She laid her hand on his cheek and gazed up at him imploringly. "You won't hurt me."

Unable to resist another second of this agonizing temptation, he grabbed her by the hand and led her to the bed. "You're wrong about that, lass. Let's go and see."

Mairi nearly stumbled over her feet as she followed Logan into the shadows. Heart racing with a mixture of excitement and panic—was she mad to be doing this?—she felt her eyes grow wide as he whirled her around next to his bed, pulled her up against the rock-hard wall of his body, crushed her mouth with his, and thrust his tongue inside.

She pressed her open palms against his chest and pushed him away. "Stop. You're just trying to scare me, prove yourself right."

"Aye, and if you know what's good for you, you'll run out of here." He stepped forward again, pulled her tight up against him, and pressed hot, open-mouthed kisses down the side of her neck.

To her complete and utter surprise, Mairi felt no further inclination to discourage him—she wanted him desperately— even though he appeared dangerously out-of-control with desire for her. His lips and tongue ate hungrily at her neck, suckling and kissing as he groaned with need, while she groped at his neck and kissed him hard on the mouth in return.

The sensations sent a flood of tingling gooseflesh down to her toes. She tilted her head back and sighed with pleasure, marveling at her unexpected willingness to give him free rein.

His good hand stroked upwards from the small of her back to her nape, where he massaged the sensitive flesh with the pad of his thumb. This relaxed her into a state of blissful enchant-ment. Then he withdrew his tongue and thrust inside again.

A pleasurable tension erupted in every corner of her being, in places she'd believed were lost forever. She cupped his face in her hands and felt a tear spill across her cheek.

Gradually, Logan eased off the violence of the kiss, and his mouth gentled. Closing his eyes, he rested his forehead against hers and inhaled deeply.

"I cannot resist you, lass."

"You don't have to."

He swallowed hard and paused a moment while her heart raced with anticipation.

"I'll do my best not to hurt you," he whispered, surrendering at last to what she wanted. Her body warmed with gratification.

She responded by climbing onto the bed, lying on her side, and beckoning for him to join her.

For a long while, he stood over her—tall, muscular, and devastatingly handsome in the golden lamplight. She didn't know what was about to occur and what he would do next, but so far, she had no regrets.

Logan reached behind his head, removed the sling that bound his arm to his ribs, and lay down on his good side, fac-ing her. "I wish I had two good hands to hold you with, lass, not just one."

"One will do fine," she replied, feeling arousal grow in her body.

Leaning closer, he kissed her again, then rolled smoothly on top of her, pinning her to the bed beneath his large, heavy body. An unexpected surge of panic swept through her at the sense of being trapped, but it subsided easily as she became lost in the pleasure of his slow, intoxicating kiss.

He leaned on his good arm and rested his other on her hip where he stroked her with the backs of his fingers. He used his mouth masterfully, kissing her cheeks, her chin, neck, and across her bare collarbone. The pleasurable, pulsing heat between her legs intensified, which affected her breathing.

At long last, his open hand slid up her quivering belly—on top of the fabric of her shift—where he paused briefly just below the rise of her breast. Then he drew back and met her gaze.

His eyes locked on hers as the fingers of his broken arm glided upward over her nipple. He stroked the firm peak with the pad of his thumb, which caused her to suck in a breath of shock and delight.

"It feels good," she whispered, trying not to compare this to her last experience five years ago. She mustn't think of that. She must purge it from her mind.

Closing her eyes, she took a few deep breaths, not realizing that her fists had clenched.

Logan's hand slid downward again and he rested his splinted arm on her belly, laid his head on the pillow.

Feeling as if she were being studied, she opened her eyes to look at him. "Why are you stopping?"

"Because you're anxious."

"I'm fine."

"Nay, you're not." He made no move to continue. "Let's just lie here together," he suggested, rolling onto his back and holding out his arm to invite her closer.

Mairi snuggled into him and rested her cheek on his shoulder. "I did like it. I didn't want you to stop."

"Just rest for a while," he said.

It wasn't long before Mairi's body relaxed into his, and she draped her leg over his thick, muscular thigh. Her hand wandered curiously over the muscles of his chest, where she explored the firm flesh and the pebbled peaks of his nipples beneath his shirt. Her breathing grew slow and heavy. Logan's did the same.

His eyes were closed, but she knew he was awake, for he was stroking her shoulder with the back of his thumb.

Feeling wonderfully aroused, Mairi leaned up on an elbow. Slowly...leisurely...she glided her hand all over his upper body—from his broad chest to his shoulder, down the length of his arm, and across to his flat stomach, where his shirt was tucked into his kilt.

Seeing the outline of his erection beneath the woolen folds, she carefully slid her hand downward to touch him there, on top of the fabric. He was shockingly large.

A breath hitched in his throat as she stroked him, then ventured beneath it to touch his hot, rigid flesh.

"*Mairi,*" he softly groaned.

"Show me how to please you," she whispered. "I need you to tell me because I don't know anything."

"Like this." He wrapped his hand around hers and directed her movements. "That's right, lass..."

A muscle flicked at his jaw and his eyes fell closed. She gloried in the power she had over him, sending him into a trance-like state. Perhaps this was what she needed—to seek pleasure by touching *him*.

Leaning over him, she pressed her mouth to his and thrust her tongue inside.

Logan tried to sit up and roll onto her again, but she pushed him back down on the bed and straddled him. "Don't move." She tugged the bottom of her shift and moved his kilt out of the way until their genitals touched. Then she rubbed herself along the length of his erection, stroking him up and down, just like he showed her how to do with her hand.

"You're slick and ready for me, lass," he whispered, sliding his hand between her legs. She rose up higher on her knees, resting above him on all fours. "I want to be inside you, but I cannot give you a child."

"That's not what I want," she assured him breathlessly, but her words turned to a whisper at the unexpected stroke of his finger along her damp center. Almost instantly, a remarkable, bewitching fever settled into her mind and she closed her eyes to revel in the decadence of erotic sensation.

His hand was like some sort of magic potion, filling her with need. Then his finger slid inside her…in and out. Soon, she was thrusting her hips to intensify the pleasure and sighing with ravenous delight. A shiver moved through her, building like a frothy wave on the ocean, gaining speed and strength as it moved toward the shoreline. It reached a crashing peak and sensation exploded within her. She quivered and cried out, collapsing on top of Logan and clinging to him with a great rush of release.

For a long time she lay there, waiting for her heartbeat to slow down while he ran his hand up and down her back, almost lulling her to sleep. She must have dozed off, she wasn't sure. Perhaps an hour had gone by. When her eyes fluttered open, Logan was sound asleep.

Feeling weary but sated—and immensely satisfied to have reached such a state of sexual gratification—she carefully rolled off him, slid off the bed, and picked up her shawl.

"Good-night, lass," Logan said in a quiet voice.

She jumped with surprise and looked down at him. "I'm sorry, Logan. I thought you were asleep."

"I was, but I'm a light sleeper." He watched her intensely in the dim lantern light. "So is that it, then?" he asked. "You come in here, have your wicked way with me, then sneak out without so much as a thank you or goodnight?"

Mairi stammered. "I'm sorry...I didn't..."

Logan chuckled softly. "I'm teasing you, lass. You can go if you like. It's probably best. But I'll expect flowers in the morning."

Mairi grinned and shyly glanced down at her feet. "Forgive me. I don't know how to do any of this."

"Nor do I," he replied, leaning up on his good arm.

She gathered her shawl more snugly about her shoulders. "I hope I'm not leaving you...unsatisfied."

He shrugged. "I'm all right."

An awkward silence ensued. Mairi cleared her throat.

"Well then..." She pointed a thumb toward the house. "I should go now and leave you to get some sleep." She tiptoed toward the door, but he called out to her.

"Mairi?"

The sound of her name upon his lips filled her with a strange mixture of ecstasy and sorrow, for she knew this was the end. It had been astonishingly wonderful, but he would be gone in the morning.

She stopped and turned.

"Did you enjoy what we did?" he asked.

Her belly fluttered with excitement at the mere mention of it. "Aye, I enjoyed it very much. Did you?"

"Aye. But I won't lie. You *have* left me wanting more."

She was quick to reply. "You could always stay another day."

He tilted his head at her and grinned. "You're a very bad influence, Mairi."

She regarded him carefully and felt a true and honest concern for the welfare of his soul. "To the contrary, I believe I could be a very *good* influence on you, Logan—if I could convince you to live for the future, not the past."

He offered no reply. He simply watched her in the open doorway until she backed out and left him alone, praying that she had not overstepped herself, and that he would still be there in the morning when she woke.

CHAPTER
NINE

⟨⟩

Logan was indeed there in the morning, knocking on the front door of the cottage and offering to take Hamish hunting for rabbits if they would be kind enough to allow him to stay another night.

Naturally, they agreed, and Mairi spent the day cleaning the cottage from top to bottom with a vitality that left Isla speechless.

The hunting expedition was a resounding success. Logan and Hamish returned late in the afternoon with two fat rabbits and plenty of stories to tell, as Hamish had done much of the work on account of Logan's broken arm.

Mairi insisted that Logan rest his arm. She skinned the rabbits herself for supper, which turned out to be the most delicious meal she'd had in ages.

⟨⟩

Three days passed, and each morning when he woke, Logan couldn't bring himself to leave the pleasures of the cozy cottage in the glen—which included the company and conversation of two good women, a keen young lad who looked up to him and was eager to learn about all the things Logan was best at, and hot meals each night.

Most importantly, he couldn't possibly quit the warm bed in Mairi's stable, where she came to him each night after the others were asleep.

Those hours that he spent with her felt like something out of a dream. They were pure bliss, and he woke each morning wondering if it had been real, for she appeared each night like an angel over his bed. Slowly, without a word, she undressed him, then she removed her shift and lay down naked beside him in the dim glow of the lamplight, where she spent the next hour exploring his body with her soft hands and warm mouth. They clung together in the darkness—touching, fondling, kissing, and sometimes talking. Her skin was always scorching hot next to his, yet he relaxed into it, and relished the firm rubdowns she gave when she turned him over onto his stomach.

She asked him what he liked sexually, and she did everything he described. She used her mouth and hands and brought him to orgasm multiple times each night.

He, in turn, pleasured her in ways he never thought he was capable of—for he never pushed to make love to her. He managed somehow to remain in control of his compulsions, and used his hands and mouth instead. Only once did he come close to penetration. He rolled on top of her and she wrapped her legs around his hips while she kissed him passionately.

Distracted and lost in sensation, Logan pushed forward, but felt the muscles of her womanhood contract. She squirmed beneath him, inching upward toward the pillow.

"I'm sorry, lass," he whispered, sitting back on his haunches. "I thought you might be ready."

She swallowed uneasily. "I thought I might be, too. Could we try it again?"

He considered her offer—which sounded more like a plea—but recognized the emotion in her eyes. It was not passion he saw, but distress. She regretted disappointing him and he knew that if they tried again, it would be for *his* pleasure, not hers.

"No," he firmly said, shaking his head. "I don't want you to pretend you're enjoying it if you're not."

"But I *am* enjoying this," she assured him.

"I believe you, lass, but you might not feel the same way when I'm thrusting into you."

Was he insane? He'd never been so sensitive to a lassie's feelings before. He enjoyed sex and he'd always pursued eager, easy lassies. He'd never in his life taken anyone's virginity. That would have been too much of a commitment. Though Mairi was not a virgin, she may as well have been, for this was a new beginning for her—and completely unfamiliar territory for him. And he had never been a patient man before—not about anything.

Mairi lay her head down on the pillow and rested her cheek on her hands. "Every night when I walk out of here, I'm afraid you'll be gone when I wake and I'll wish I had let you make love to me."

"I won't leave without saying good-bye to you and Hamish," he told her, as he ran a finger across her soft cheek.

"But you *will* leave eventually," she said. "And probably very soon. I can feel it in my bones. I know you're thinking about it."

Logan could do nothing but nod his head. "I must go after my brother. For one thing, I owe him a wicked thrashing for what he did to my sword arm. But in truth, my anger has waned. He had every right to do what he did. I cannot desert him. I owe him my life."

At least he hadn't lied to Mairi about his continuing desire to leave. Perhaps there was hope for him yet.

They fell asleep in each other's arms, and as usual, when he woke the following morning, she was gone, back to her own bed.

But something was different that day, for he was awakened not by the glare of the sun through the window, but by the sound of a horse galloping into the yard and a man's deep resounding voice as he dismounted. Boots hit the ground with a heavy thud.

"Good morning, Mairi. You're up early."

It was a Scottish accent, not English. But who was it?

Logan leapt to his feet and dressed quickly.

"Who is this?" the Highlander asked incredulously, reaching for his sword as Logan walked out of the stable.

"His name is Logan," Mairi quickly explained. She was fully dressed with the empty milk bucket in her hand.

"Logan MacDonald," he offered, striding forward and holding out his good hand.

Tomas glanced at Logan's clan tartan and brooch and stiffened with displeasure, for there was age-old bad blood between the Campbells and MacDonalds.

"He's a guest, Tomas," Mairi added. "As you can see, he's injured. We've been giving him care."

The man she called Tomas was a tall, strapping beast of a Scot with shoulder-length red hair, a beard, and more weapons tucked into his belt than any crofter had a right to claim.

This one was a seasoned warrior, no doubt about it.

"Logan, this is Tomas Campbell," Mairi said, gesturing toward him. "He's a *friend*."

Logan regarded the man suspiciously. Though he looked to be about twenty years older than Mairi, he was good looking—muscular and fit with friendly blue eyes. Clearly she was at ease in his presence.

In Logan's experience, whenever a woman made a point to say that a man was a "friend," there was something not right about it. Logan felt a sudden, unwelcome stab of jealousy.

"Good to meet you," he said nonetheless as he shook Tomas's hand. They regarded each other with a masculine intensity, neither wanting to be the first to look away.

"You're a MacDonald..." Tomas said with a hint of menace. "What are you doing in Campbell territory?"

"It's a long story," Mairi replied, touching Logan's arm. For some reason, the tension grew thick as mud.

Just then, the front door of the house swung open and Isla walked out. "Tomas! How wonderful to see you! Can you stay for breakfast? I've got eggs in the pan and a fresh loaf of bread on the table. It's still warm."

The mistrust in Tomas's eyes vanished as he turned to greet Mairi's mother. "You certainly know the way to a man's heart, Isla. I could smell the bread from clear across the glen."

He kissed Isla on the cheek.

Mairi met Logan's gaze. The sun reflected in her pupils like a flash of starlight. She raised an eyebrow.

Any jealousy he'd been feeling disappeared like a drop of water on a hot stove, for Tomas was obviously there to visit Isla.

"You come with news," she said with a sudden look of concern. "Something's happened. I see it in your eyes."

"Aye," Tomas replied gruffly. "There have been some developments at Leathan Castle. We'd best go inside."

Logan's gut turned over with regret for having been convalescing here for so long, while Darach had been out there alone with Fitzroy Campbell's daughter, fulfilling their mission faithfully.

An inexplicable feeling of dread came over Logan as he followed everyone into the cottage to hear the news Tomas had come to deliver.

⟨⟡⟩

Isla poured coffee for Tomas and Logan while Mairi served up the eggs.

"Hamish, put your toy away," she whispered, urging her son to get up off the floor and join the men at the table.

A moment later they were all seated, and Tomas wasted no time before getting straight to the point of why he had come. "Chief Fitzroy Campbell is dead."

Isla dropped her fork, and Logan sat back in his chair, dumbfounded.

For the past two years he had lived for vengeance, dreaming of the day he would kill Fitzroy with his own bare hands, but now he was dead.

"How?" Logan asked.

Had Darach not arrived at the castle in time to deliver the pardon to save Fitzroy's life? Had something happened to Darach along the way?

"Believe it or not," Tomas said, "Fitzroy escaped from the prison a few nights ago and was shot by a company of English Redcoats in the forest, half a day's ride from the castle."

"Good heavens," Mairi said with a frown of disbelief. "How in the world did he escape?"

"That's the interesting part." Tomas scooped up a fried egg and stuffed the entire thing into his mouth. "It was his daughter, Larena, who broke him out of the prison with the help of a Highlander from Kinloch Castle, who had escorted her into the garrison to deliver her father's pardon from the King. Some say the Highlander kidnapped her and her father, but that makes no sense."

Mairi and Isla both turned to Logan and stared at him with shock and bewilderment, for they both knew he had been on a mission with his brother to deliver a "package" from Kinloch to Leathan Castle. Now they must be guessing what that package was, and surely they must be wondering why Logan was allegedly involved in a plot to help a Jacobite traitor escape.

Not just any Jacobite traitor, but the Campbell chief they both abhorred.

But that had not been his plan. Not at all. It was quite the opposite in fact.

"How do you know this?" Logan asked Tomas.

"I have friends inside the castle walls. Word spreads quickly."

Logan waited for Isla or Mairi to say something to Tomas—to expose the fact that he had been on the same mission from Kinloch Castle when he ended up in their field with a broken arm, on account of his brother.

Thankfully, neither of them spoke a word about it. They were likely still in shock.

"What about Larena and the Highlander?" Logan asked incredulously. "What happened to them?"

"The Highlander was shot dead on the spot," Tomas replied, "and they dragged the chief's daughter back to the garrison. They say she will be forced to marry Colonel Gregory Chatham, as she was pledged to him in exchange for the pardon on her father's life—although a lot of good that did her. I don't know why she tried to break her father out of prison when he was already spared from the gallows, but who knows what she was thinking? Now she has no choice in the matter. She'll be trading her virtue on her wedding night for the crime she just committed against the Crown."

Tomas smeared cheese on his bread and continued his tirade. "I hate to say it—because she's the daughter of that blackguard Fitzroy Campbell and I should hate her by association—but I pity her. From what I've heard, Colonel Chatham is a cowardly whoremonger. He's rather twisted, they say."

Meanwhile, Logan was hearing none of what Tomas was saying about Larena Campbell or Colonel Chatham, for he was still reeling from the news that Darach had been shot and killed.

The room began to spin, and his vision turned red before his eyes. He stood up and knocked his chair over.

Darach. *Dead*?

The next thing Logan knew, he was pushing out the front door of the cottage, stripping the sling off his shoulder, tossing it to the ground and running toward the stable. He was vaguely aware of Mairi calling after him.

He wrenched open the stable door and entered the stall where his horse was waiting dutifully, as if he knew Logan would come eventually and expect him to gallop.

Blood pounded thunderously in Logan's ears as he mounted Tracker, bareback, and urged him out of the stall.

Mairi appeared in the open doorway. "Wait Logan! *Please wait!*"

Unable to get by her, Tracker backed up a few steps and whinnied anxiously.

"Out of the way, Mairi. I have to go."

She held her hands up to try and stop him. "What will you do? If you ride through the gates of Leathan Castle, you'll be shot dead on the spot, just like your brother. You must think this through."

But he didn't want to *think*. He just wanted to ride out of there and find the soldier who killed Darach.

"Please, Logan, don't go. *Stay!*"

"I cannot!" His body was on fire with rage and a crushing need to retaliate. *What man had pulled the trigger? What was his name? What did he look like?* It was all Logan cared about. "Move out of the way, Mairi!"

She stepped aside and he kicked in his heels.

Ten minutes later, he was riding fast and hard to the edge of the grassy glen, leaning forward over Tracker's mane and shouting at him to gallop faster. *Faster!*

Then it hit Logan like a cold, crashing wave.

Darach was dead.

Grief, like nothing Logan had ever known, washed over him.

His brother, who had been his only family since he was a lad…the brother who had protected him and saved him from certain death on the battlefield of Sheriffmuir…*Darach*, who had kept Logan's shameful secret all these years…was dead.

Logan sat back and tugged on Tracker's mane. "Whoa!"

Tracker slowed to a halt at the river, where the water rushed noisily over the rocks. The morning sun, just rising from beyond the mountaintops, blinded Logan momentarily. He squinted and raised a hand to shield his eyes from the glare.

Only then did he realize that his wounded arm was throbbing like a son of a bitch.

Darach was dead.

Feeling nauseous, Logan dismounted and retched into the grass next to a large, granite boulder. When he recovered, he lay down on his back, closed his eyes and covered them with his splinted arm.

Where was he going? What would he do?

God, Mairi was right. He would be shot instantly if he rode into the British garrison in a blaze of fury and vengeance. And how would that make things better? It wouldn't bring Darach back to life. Nor would it bring back their father.

Dear God, what had they done with Darach's body? Had he at least been given a proper burial?

Larena...it was all her fault. How had she convinced Darach to break her father out of prison? Darach loathed her father. Was the pardon on his life not enough? Larena wanted his freedom as well? Had she wanted it enough to put Darach's life at risk in the process?

Poor Darach...no doubt seduced into doing her bidding. He'd probably fancied himself in love with her and had lost sight of everything, for he had tried to rescue a man who had murdered their own father in cold blood.

Still lying on the grass, Logan gazed up at the clear blue morning sky. At least Larena—damn her treacherous soul—would spend her life wed to the twisted English officer who was responsible for her father's death. Was that not a suitable punishment? It was a rather perfect end to her story, for there was some justice in that.

What was Logan to do, then? he wondered miserably as he lay there, feeling numb and lost. For so long, he had lived for his dark vengeance. Now he was alone in this world with nothing—and no one—to live for.

But no...that wasn't right. There was Mairi...beautiful Mairi...who had tried to keep him from leaving. She had wanted him to stay—to save his soul—but he had ridden off in a rage and left her, just like he'd ridden out of the camp after his fight with Darach.

What was Mairi doing now? Logan wondered in a hazy, despairing stupor. Was she worrying for him? Or was she explaining to Tomas that he had been a part of the mission to deliver the King's pardon to Leathan Castle? Was she telling him that Logan was the brother of the Highlander who had been killed, and that he had galloped off in a fury and could not be trusted?

CHAPTER

ELEVEN

Mairi paced across the floor of the stable, not knowing what to do. If only she had a horse of her own, she would ride after Logan and convince him to turn around and think more carefully about what he should do.

Now she understood why he'd ended up on his back in her field with a broken arm a week ago. He was rash and impulsive, and had galloped away from his brother's camp without a saddle for his horse, or any of his weapons. That's why he was unable to complete his mission—which she now understood was to deliver the pardon to save Fitzroy Campbell, and escort his daughter Larena back to the castle.

Clearly, Larena Campbell was the woman Darach and Logan had argued about.

Tomas and Isla ran into the stable.

"Did he leave?" Tomas asked.

"Aye," Mairi replied. "He was fit to be tied. The man you told us about—the Highlander who was shot by the Redcoats—he was Logan's brother. Logan also comes from Kinloch. He was on a mission for Angus the Lion to deliver Fitzroy Campbell's pardon from the king."

"I know," Tomas said. "Isla told me everything. Which way did he go?"

Mairi pointed. "That way. I suspect he's riding straight for Leathan Castle as we speak, but he won't amount to much with a broken arm and no weapons."

"The lad needs to be stopped or he'll get himself killed," Tomas said as he strode out of the stable and mounted his horse.

Mairi followed him out. "He's a good man, Tomas. He's just...*passionate*. Please bring him back."

"I'll knock his lights out and drag him back by the ear if I have to," Tomas replied as he galloped out of the yard.

⋘⋙

Logan was on his feet and ready to mount Tracker when he heard the predictable sound of hooves thundering across the glen. He was not surprised to discover Tomas approaching.

"Mairi must have sent you," Logan said as Tomas reached him and reined his horse to a halt. Logan swung himself up onto Tracker's back.

"Aye," Tomas replied. "She was worried about you."

Logan regarded the red-bearded Highlander with careful scrutiny. "I cannot blame her. She knows I'm reckless."

Yet he had surprised himself by demonstrating an astonishing degree of self-control over the past week—at least where Mairi was concerned.

"The word she used was *passionate*," Tomas informed him. His horse stomped around skittishly, while Logan hugged his broken arm to his ribs.

"And Isla told me that you're a scout for Angus the Lion, and that you were on an errand, traveling to Leathan to deliver some sort of 'package' when you got into a brawl with your brother."

"Aye," Logan replied, feeling weary of lies. "And if you know that much, I suspect you've already figured out that it was my brother the Redcoats killed."

Tomas nodded and spoke in a low, gentle voice. "My condolences, son. It's never easy to lose a brother."

Logan lowered his gaze to the ground. "Nay, it is not."

"What will you do now?" Tomas asked, after a time. "Mairi is hoping I'll bring you back. And seeing as you have no weapons and no saddle for your horse, it's probably best for you to come with me now. Then you can take some time to put some thought into where you should go from here."

Logan exhaled heavily and looked toward the horizon. "I have no idea where that is. My world is not the same as it was."

I don't even know who I am anymore. MacDonald? Campbell?

"I know the feeling," Tomas said. "It's been a rough few years for us Campbells, since the death of our true chief."

Logan's gut churned with burning acid, for it was his own beloved father Tomas was referring to. But no one knew that—not even Mairi. Darach had been the only person in the world who knew the truth. And now he was gone.

Logan had never felt more alone.

And so, with nowhere to go and all his goals shattered, he soberly followed Tomas back to Mairi's cottage, and surrendered completely to his grief.

⬥

Logan wasn't sure why he was so surprised to find Mairi waiting outside for him when he walked his horse into the yard. She must have been watching from the window.

His feet barely had a chance to hit the ground before she dashed into his arms and pressed her cheek to his chest. He cupped her head in his good hand and whispered, "It's all right, lass. I've come to my senses."

"Thank God," she whispered, looking up into his eyes and causing him to wonder how he could ever have ridden away from her. "I'm sorry about your brother."

Hamish ran out of the house, without understanding what was happening. They must have shielded him from the truth. "Logan! You're back! Can we go hunting for rabbits today?"

Mairi quickly wiped a tear from her cheek and turned to speak gently to her son. "Logan can't go hunting today, darling. He's had some bad news. Why don't you go inside and help Grammy sweep out the hearth."

"All right," he said dejectedly, returning to the house with Tomas.

Mairi faced Logan again and spoke with purpose. "Please let me take you away from here. We'll go for a ride, just the two of us."

Logan was keenly aware of Isla meeting Tomas and Hamish at the door and beckoning them inside—and the closing of the door behind them.

"Aye," Logan agreed, taking Mairi by the arm and leading her to his horse. He mounted first, then held out his good arm to hoist her up behind him. She wrapped her hands around his waist and they galloped out of the yard together, across the back field, toward the forest.

❦

"This is the place," Logan said, urging Tracker to a halt in the sunlit glade. "This is where Darach and I got into the fight that would turn out to be our last."

He felt a sudden stabbing sensation in his heart.

"What *really* happened here?" Mairi asked, looking around at the evidence of their stopover in the glade—the charred remains of the campfire and the saddle that had been left behind, so carelessly. "You told me there was a woman involved, but I had no idea it was Larena Campbell—that *she* was the package you were delivering, along with the pardon. I assumed it was some sort of love triangle, a disagreement over a woman back at Kinloch."

Logan knelt down on one knee before his saddle and ran his fingertips over the smooth, polished leather. "I don't even know where to begin, Mairi. There's so much I haven't told you." He bowed his head and closed his eyes. "Secrets. It's all very complicated."

She slowly strolled closer and approached him from behind. "My life is complicated, too. At least I've always imagined it to be. You've been very patient with me over the past week, Logan, and you've proven yourself trustworthy. If you choose to confide in me, I owe you no less than that. Whatever you tell me, I give you my word that I will not betray your confidence."

Logan rose to his feet and faced her. "You may regret that promise, Mairi, when you find out who I really am."

"I've been lying to you from the start," he said. "My name is not Logan MacDonald. It's Logan Campbell."

Her eyebrows drew together with confusion. "But you told us you hail from Kinloch Castle, and you dress in MacDonald tartan. Why would Angus the Lion allow you to be a scout and trust you with such an important errand if you were not a member of his clan?"

"Because I've been masquerading as a MacDonald since I was eleven years old. Darach and I, both. Angus never knew who we really were. He thought we were a couple of MacDonald orphans."

"But why would you leave your own clan for another?"

"I told you…" He bowed his head. "It's complicated."

"Then maybe you should start at the beginning?"

Logan strode to the campfire—it was nothing but scorched wood and ash now—and suggested that Mairi sit down.

She sank to her knees while he remained on his feet.

"Are you aware of the story I told Hamish about the two brothers on the battlefield," Logan asked, "and the younger one who was afraid?"

"Aye, he spoke of it," she replied.

Logan paced around the glade, not wanting to meet Mairi's gaze. "There was truth in it. I was the foolish boy who snuck away to follow his brave older brother off to war. Darach wasn't pleased. When the battle began, I was terrified and regretted following him, but of course I didn't tell him that. I pretended I wanted to be there, but he was always very protective of me."

Logan stopped pacing. "When he broke my arm here in this very place, it was not the first time he'd done something like that. Shortly after the English cannons started firing at Sheriffmuir, he clubbed me over the head and carried me off."

Mairi's eyebrows pulled together with bewilderment. "You deserted?"

"Aye. But it was worse than that. A fellow clansman found us afterward and drew his sword to force us to return and face our punishment. He said we were cowards and should hang. When Darach refused to go with him, things got out of control. Darach was forced to defend us both and he wounded the man, who probably would have reported us if a Redcoat hadn't appeared out of the bush and finished him off with a bayonet. Darach always blamed himself for that clansman's death."

"Good heavens."

"We left him there and hid in the woods until the next morning. We knew that if we ever showed our faces at Leathan Castle again, there would be a price on our heads and our father would be disgraced. We couldn't allow that to happen because he was an important man. We were very ashamed."

"Who was your father?" Mairi asked.

Logan faced her squarely and spoke the words out loud for the first time in fifteen years. "My father was Ronald James Campbell. Former laird of Leathan Castle."

All the color drained from Mairi's face as she stared at Logan in disbelief. "The clan believes that he died with no heirs."

"That's right, lass. *He* believed it, too. He thought we perished during the battle, along with his other sons, our older brothers—although I suspect, since our bodies could not have been found, that he always held out hope." Logan pressed his fist to his chest and pounded it over his heart. "And that is the shame and guilt I have carried inside me all my life, lass. I'd always wanted to go home, to reconcile with my father…tell him how sorry I was. I would have taken whatever punishment he wished to impose upon me. Even death. I always assumed that one day, when the time was right and I could convince Darach to go, we would return and confess the truth to him. But then he was murdered."

Mairi rose to her feet. "So the man who was the target of your vengeance was Fitzroy Campbell, Larena's father? Because you believed he orchestrated your father's death?"

Logan turned away and watched the water bubble gently over the rocks. "Aye. I thought, if I could avenge my father's death, he would know somehow from beyond the grave that I had redeemed myself, and he would be proud. Then I would have been absolved of this wretched guilt and shame. *That* is why I wanted to reach Leathan—so that I could kill my father's murderer with my own hands before the English had a chance to hang him."

"But Darach didn't want you to do that," Mairi said, rising to her feet and striding toward him. "He wanted you to lay the past to rest."

"Aye." Logan sat down on the bank of the creek and stretched his legs out in front of him. "But now Darach is gone, too, and there is no one left who shares this guilt and shame with me, no one who truly understands it. Justice seems pointless now that everyone is gone. And it's *my* fault Darach is dead. If I hadn't been so impatient, I would have been at his side at Leathan Castle. I would have talked him out of helping Fitzroy escape from prison. I wouldn't have let him become *bewitched* by the daughter of our enemy."

Mairi sat down beside Logan and spoke heatedly. "His death is not your fault. He was a grown man and only he can be responsible for his actions. You weren't even there, Logan."

He lay down on the grass and pressed the heels of his hands to his forehead. "You should leave me here, Mairi," he said. "Go back to your family. I'm not worthy of you."

The very next instant, she was lying beside him, dropping sweet, soothing kisses on his cheeks and neck.

"What are you doing?" he asked, not wanting this. Not now.

"Please let me comfort you." She pulled his face toward her and kissed him tenderly on the mouth while she lifted her knee across his thigh. He felt an instant stirring of arousal, and was strangely grateful for it—for it drowned out all the thoughts of his brother, all the pain and the stinging regrets that were crashing around like thunder in his heart.

The heat of her slender form caused him to draw in a quick breath. She was too close, too lush, and the natural womanly fragrance of her body was an aphrodisiac in his nostrils.

"You shouldn't be doing this, Mairi," he said in a gruff voice. "I have no strength left. I'm weary and all broken up inside. I won't be able to resist what you're offering. Not this time."

She leaned up on an elbow and looked down at him with love and sympathy. "You don't need to resist anything, Logan. Just let me hold you."

And so he did. For a long while she snuggled close and pressed her body tightly to his, kissing him on the cheek and sharing in his grief. "I'm so sorry, Logan," she kept saying, while the water rushed passed them in the creek and birds soared high in the sky overhead. Logan closed his eyes and tried to let the sounds of nature replace the deafening noise of sorrow and regret in his head.

Then Mairi slid her hand across his chest, down over his torso, and lower to the top of his kilt. She stroked him for a moment on top of the thick fabric, then slid her hand underneath.

Though it felt wrong and selfish to allow her to continue, Logan made no effort to stop her, for he wanted to lose himself in physical sensation, so that he could forget who he was and what he'd learned on this unbearable day. He shut his eyes and a tear spilled across his cheek. Mairi leaned close to kiss it away, then she rolled on top of him and straddled him on the grass.

Gazing up at her in the shimmering morning light, Logan marveled at her beauty and her soft, gentle form, then he cupped her hips in his hands while she tugged at her skirts, hurrying to push them out of the way and raise his kilt.

No...this wasn't the right time. She shouldn't be doing this...

She shifted her bottom around and gently—though decisively—took him all the way into her damp, heated depths.

Logan groaned in ecstasy, though perhaps it was a sob of grief that escaped him.

"*Shh,*" Mairi whispered, moving slowly. "Just let yourself go."

She moved in such a way, little by little, up and down, that it was difficult to hold out. The pleasure was overpowering and his body began to shudder. He gripped her hips tightly, flipped her over onto her back, rolled onto her and pushed harder and deeper, again and again, for as long as he could until all his thoughts dissolved into nothingness and his bones melted into a strange, agonizing rapture. He continued to make love to her, resisting the imminent peak until heat poured through him and he shuddered violently above her, shooting his seed into her womb without a single care for the consequences.

She held him tight and whispered loving words in his ear. *"It's all right now. I'm here. It's all right now."*

A mourning dove cooed somewhere in the treetops.

"Are you sorry?" he carefully asked when he recovered himself and drew back to look down at her face. "Did I hurt you?"

"No, you did not hurt me. I wanted to feel close to you. I *still* want it."

"I'm here, lass," he said, gathering her close, "and I'm not going anywhere."

Where had that come from?

Did he truly mean it?

A sudden burst of emotion flashed across her face and her chin trembled.

He wasn't sure if he'd said the wrong thing and made her sad, or was she happy? None of this was in his normal realm of experience. He had never needed a woman like this, never felt so completely involved and grateful for all that she was—her kindness and virtue—and for all that she was willing to give to help make him feel whole again.

And to heal herself, he supposed.

"Don't cry," he said, stroking her cheek with the pad of his thumb. "What's wrong, love?"

She shook her head and fought back tears, then sat up and regarded him with apprehension. "I don't know. I didn't say anything before, but perhaps I should have."

Logan sat up, too, and frowned at her. "About what?" His stomach turned over with dread.

"About Tomas. There is something you don't know about him." Mairi paused and wet her lips before she found the courage to continue. She reached out and touched Logan's arm. "He knew your father. He was close to him. He loved him like a brother."

A suffocating sensation tightened around Logan's throat. "*How* did he know him? I don't remember him."

She took a deep breath and let it out slowly. "They met on the battlefield at Sheriffmuir, for he lost his sons that day, too. After it was over, they searched together. Tomas found both his boys lying dead, together at the front of the line."

Logan bowed his head as he considered this. "*Oh, God.* If he learns what Darach and I did, he will think us the worst cowards in the world."

"No, you mustn't think that." She sat up on her knees. "We've known Tomas forever. His sister is our neighbor and he is a good, kind man. I've heard him say dozens of times that he wished his sons had fled and refused to fight that day, because what was it all for? He once spoke about the laird's grief over the loss of his sons, and how Tomas wished they could be found, or that they would return. He wished they were saved somehow, that they had survived to fight another day. Now here you are."

All the breath sailed out of Logan's lungs and he rose to his feet. "He cannot know the truth, Mairi. I should leave here this minute and never come back."

"No, don't say such a thing!" she shouted. "You've told me the truth and I understand. Tomas will understand, too. You are the son of Ronald James Campbell and you were *eleven years old* on that battlefield! You cannot go back to Kinloch and continue to live a lie. You must stay here. With us. With *me*."

"And do what with my life?" Logan demanded to know, spreading his arms wide while the familiar, heavy mantle of shame settled back upon his shoulders.

Mairi strode toward him and spoke calmly, in a soft voice. "Just *love* me. That's all."

He shook his head at her. "And continue to live with my dishonor?"

"There is no dishonor," she firmly said. "You were just a boy. I see nothing in you to be ashamed of. All I see now is a man with regrets, and we all have regrets, Logan. That is life. We make mistakes. But we must learn from them and forge ahead, grab hold of whatever joy we can find. Don't you agree? We could have a good life here, you and me. We could be very happy."

Logan regarded Mairi in the morning light and marveled yet again at her inconceivable goodness and innocence.

Aye, he could be very happy with Mairi Campbell. He could easily spend the rest of his days doing everything in his power to make her happy in return.

To love her.

Protect her.

To sharing her bed each night and teach her about pleasures she's never known or imagined.

Was that it, then? Was *this* his destiny? Had it been his destiny all along to return to Campbell territory, find this woman and let go of his thirst for vengeance? And to let go of his brother and father, who were already lost to him?

Was he to lay down his sword, leave the warrior life behind, and become a crofter? Take a wife and raise a family?

"It's too much, Mairi," he said, telling the truth, at least. "I've lived my life for one purpose alone. To atone for what I did, and to avenge my father's murder. Despite the lies, I've been a loyal, dedicated scout for Angus the Lion. I am a trained warrior."

She strode closer. "We can discover a *new* purpose for you. We can discover it together. Over time."

He looked away, but she laid a hand on his cheek and forced him to meet her gaze. "Do you not care for me enough?" she asked. "Is that it? Please be honest with me, Logan. You owe me that much."

"I care for you a great deal, Mairi. More than I ever imagined I could ever care for anyone."

"Then *stay*," she pleaded. "And let us tell Tomas the truth. I give you my word that he can be trusted. He would never betray us. And perhaps, when all is said and done, he will give you the peace in your heart that you have been seeking all along."

"Peace is a foreign thing to me, lass," Logan said. "I do not think it even exists. At least not for me."

She backed away and looked at him with disappointment. "Are you saying that you intend to leave? That you cannot be happy here?"

He strode closer and took hold of her shoulder. "I'm saying nothing of the sort, lass. I've never been happier than I've been here with you. I've never known…"

"What?"

"I've never known such *hope* before. The loss of my brother has taken the wind out me, but it makes me cherish you all the more, because you let yourself love me today."

"I do love you, Logan," she insisted, "and I desire you as well. I never imagined I could feel that way about any man, but somehow you've helped to change me."

"You changed me, too, lass, and I cannot fathom the idea of leaving you."

"So you will stay?" she asked.

"Aye, and I will make you my wife, if you will have me."

Her eyes lit up with surprise and wonder. "Of course I will have you."

"But you must promise me one thing," he added.

"Anything, Logan. I will promise you anything."

"Give me your word that you will never tell a living soul what I told you today, not even Tomas, your mother, or Hamish. My name is Logan MacDonald, and I'm from Kinloch Castle. That is all anyone must ever know."

She bowed her head and hesitated to agree.

"It may be a lie," he continued, hoping to convince her that it was what he needed most from her, "but at least there is truth between the two of *us*, and that is all that matters. I require nothing else to give me peace, other than your love, Mairi. All I want is *you*."

Her eyes lifted and she rose up on her toes to wrap her arms around his neck.

When his lips touched hers, he wondered with apprehension how it could be possible for a man like him to be awarded such a gift—to be presented with such joy in the perfection of Mairi Campbell's love. Surely it could not be this easy to lay the past to rest. His brother had just been shot and killed by English Redcoats. Surely, Logan would not be able to move on from this so easily.

PART TWO

Atonement

GHIRGEEN

They were married three weeks later in a private ceremony at the base of the mountain at mid-day, when the sun was high in the sky. Aside from Isla and Hamish and the priest, the only guests in attendance were Tomas, his sister Catriona and her husband Murray, along with their two sons, who were old enough to take wives of their own, but to their mother's constant discontent, had no interest in hurrying to the altar. They were more than happy to celebrate Logan's and Mairi's special day, however, and provided ample entertainment by getting drunk on whisky and singing until the sun went down.

That night, after the celebration in the cottage, Isla and Hamish returned with Catriona and Murray to their cottage beyond the glen to give Mairi and Logan a proper wedding night in their own home.

As soon as everyone was gone, Mairi began to tidy up the kitchen, but Logan closed the front door, locked it, and took hold of her hand.

His arm was mostly healed, though he still favored it. There was no more splint.

"I'm your husband now, Mairi," he whispered in her ear as he pulled her close and began to dance slowly with her before the crackling fire, "and I must insist that there will be no drudgery on your wedding night."

She smiled up at him, laid her cheek against his warm chest and marveled at what felt like a dream come true, for he was the most loving, tender, and handsome husband.

"How is this possible?" she asked, gazing up at him in the firelight. "What did I ever do to deserve such happiness?"

"I hope I'll always make you happy, Mairi," he replied. "I hope I never disappoint you."

"You won't," she said. "I *know* you won't."

He carried her off to bed, then made love to her with extraordinary passion and tenderness until dawn. Even then, a part of her could not truly accept this unexpected gift. Life had never been this bountiful before. It seemed she'd always faced challenge and tragedy.

Perhaps there were still challenges ahead of her, for although Logan's arm had healed almost completely, she understood that he still carried a burning secret that left him broken on the inside. He grieved for his brother who had died at the hands of the English, and though Logan had been distracted by Mairi's love over the past few weeks, she suspected the hatred and the desire to avenge his father and brother would eventually return. She knew he was a warrior at heart, and if another company of English soldiers ever threatened her safety, she feared he would don his weapons and unleash the beast he'd locked inside.

She wasn't sure what she would do when that day came, or how she would convince him to remain here and live in peace, as a crofter. Would their love be enough for him? Would *she* be enough? Was this his destiny, or was there another?

Perhaps a child would fill his heart more fully than his desire for vengeance. That had certainly been the case for her. When Hamish had come along, he'd brought an extraordinary love with him that changed her life.

She said a silent, secret prayer that Logan had planted a seed in her belly that very night.

⚜

The next seven days were pure bliss for Logan, who made love to his beautiful wife each night and somehow managed to suppress thoughts of Darach's death. Perhaps it was selfish and unwise of him to distract himself from the grief, but he did so nonetheless, and Mairi never pressed him to express his feelings about it—not since the day in the glade when he confessed all his shameful secrets to her. She was surprisingly cheerful most of the time, not wanting to remind him of what he'd confided, he supposed.

He worried something would eventually happen to remind him of the truth in the world—the truth inside himself—and all of this superficial joy would come crashing down around him.

Sadly, for Mairi, that day came sooner than expected, on a rainy afternoon when Tomas rode into the yard with more news from the castle.

CHAPTER

FOURTEEN

"Are you certain? Where did you hear this?" Logan asked, rising to his feet when Tomas walked through the door, shocking them all with the information he had gleaned.

"I heard it from a cook in the kitchen at Leathan," Tomas replied. "She overheard some Redcoats discussing what had happened."

"So you are telling me that my brother *lives*? That he survived the gunshot wound and escaped with Larena?"

"Aye, lad, that's exactly what I'm telling you. My spy in the castle said that Chatham rode north in pursuit of them, for he wanted the lassie as his wife. Good luck to *him*," Tomas said, his tone dripping with sarcasm. "Sounds like she made her choice, and it was your brother."

"God help Darach," Logan said.

But at least he was alive. Darach was *alive*.

Logan sank onto the chair, cupped his hands together in front of his face, shut his eyes and whispered, "*Thank you, Lord.*" Then he looked up at Tomas again. "What else do you know?"

Tomas sat down across from him at the table while Mairi poured coffee for both of them. "From what I understand, Chatham found your brother and Larena at Kinloch Castle, but your brother escaped yet again. That occurred a few weeks ago. My spy doesn't know what happened to Larena—if she went with your brother or remained behind. We suspect she went with your brother, considering what Colonel Chatham's been up to over the past few weeks."

"What is that?" Logan asked with a frown.

Tomas's jaw clenched. He pounded his big fist on the table and caused the coffee to splash about in the cup. "He's been riding about the Highlands taking his revenge out on every last innocent Scot he comes across. He's burned out crofters, allowed his men to rape and pillage—always accusing everyone of being a Jacobite traitor. He's on a rampage. The man has to be stopped." Tomas paused. "We need our castle back. That's why I've come here, lad. I must speak with you."

"Me?" Logan glanced up at Mairi and wondered if she'd betrayed his confidence to Tomas or Isla. She shook her head at him, as if she understood his suspicion and assured him that no, she had not betrayed his trust.

"I understand that you Campbells want your castle back from the English," Logan said to Tomas, "but that's not my problem. I'm a MacDonald. I just want to find my brother."

Tomas's eyes narrowed and he spoke in a low, commanding tone. "I'm not a fool, lad. I can put two and two together and come up with four, not three."

Logan swallowed uneasily and raised the coffee cup to his lips. Working hard to maintain a calm demeanor, he took a sip, then set the cup down. "I don't know what you're referring to, Tomas."

Tomas inclined his head knowingly. "There's no point trying to hide who you are, lad. Not with me. I knew your father too well. I was his laird of war for almost a decade. We shared a bond and were friends for many years."

Logan's heart began to pound hard and fast in his chest. He spoke not a single word. He merely glared at Tomas, while Mairi stopped what she was doing at the worktable and watched them intently.

Tomas's eyes glimmered with satisfaction and he pointed at Logan. "Ach! I knew it. You are his son—the youngest, I reckon. Your resemblance to your father is uncanny. I'm surprised no one else has figured it out." Tomas glanced up in a heavenly direction. "If only Ronald were alive today to see that you survived Sheriffmuir. You and your brother both."

Logan rose to his feet. "You sound so sure of all that. But if it were so, he'd be ashamed of us. Lucky for him he's six feet under."

Mairi took a step forward. "Logan, please..."

He held up a hand and regarded Tomas with displeasure. "It seems there's no way to hide the truth now, since you already know it. Aye, I am Ronald's son, but Darach and I fled the battlefield fifteen years ago. We deserted our clan like a couple of miserable cowards. Darach nearly killed a man to keep our secret. Is that what you wanted to hear, Tomas? Is that what you think our father would have wanted to see?"

"You were just a wee lad," Tomas argued with pain in his eyes, "with no business being on an open battlefield against the English army. I don't blame you for running. I wanted to run myself."

"But you didn't," Logan said.

"Nay, but I wasn't a wee lad."

Logan took a deep breath and fought against the pulsing knot of anxiety that was churning in his gut. "Darach wasn't so young. He was fourteen."

"He was trying to protect you," Mairi put in.

Mairi paled when Logan shot a warning glance at her.

"I don't see the point in discussing any of this, Mairi, when I've finally put it behind me." He turned to Tomas. "What do you want from me?"

"I want you to help us get our castle back."

Logan scoffed and spread his arms wide. "You're asking *me*? Why? I'm a bloody nobody—a nobody who once betrayed his clan and has made an oath of allegiance to another chief of an enemy clan."

"That's exactly why you're the man we need, Logan. You pledged an oath to Angus the Lion and you've been a faithful member of his clan almost all your life. With what's been happening in the Highlands lately—namely Colonel Chatham killing innocent Scots and stirring up trouble—surely the great Lion would be willing to hear you out. If we could convince him to join forces with us and take Leathan back from the English…"

Logan laughed out loud. "The MacDonalds helping the Campbells? Are you mad? Have you forgotten what happened at Glencoe?"

Tomas waved a dismissive hand. "Ach, that's ancient history. Besides, it wasn't the Campbells of Leathan that were involved in that massacre. We had nothing to do with it. As of today, we're both on the same side, Logan—Scotland against English tyranny. Chatham has been wreaking havoc on Kinloch lands more than anywhere else because he suspects the MacDonalds helped Darach escape. I suspect Angus is chomping at the bit to call out the charge and put a battering ram through Chatham's gates."

For a moment that image lit a fire in Logan's belly—for he couldn't imagine anything more satisfying—but then he glanced at Mairi and thought about how she'd been working so hard to convince him to live a life of peace, to let go of the past. He bowed his head. "I just want to find my brother."

"You will, lad." Tomas patted Logan firmly on the shoulder. "Let me travel with you to Kinloch to speak for the Campbells of Leathan. We'll talk to your MacDonald laird together. I'm sure he knows where Darach has gone."

Logan looked at Mairi again. She stood in front of the hearth, watching him with questioning eyes.

God help him, he loved her. He truly did, but he could not stay here and do nothing while his brother was on the run from a tyrant—and that same tyrant was burning out innocent crofters and raping the women of two clans. She, of all people, should understand why he couldn't let such atrocities continue.

"When will you leave?" Mairi asked, recognizing the truth in his eyes before he spoke a word.

"Right away, I suspect." He glanced at Tomas, who nodded with approval.

"It will be dangerous," Mairi said. "If your brother helped Larena's father escape from an English prison, then they've become fugitives. Chatham will continue hunting for them—especially if Chatham is in love with Larena. He'll want to kill Darach."

Logan stood. "Which is exactly why I must leave here today and travel to Kinloch. I must find out where they went. I must see Darach again and make things right."

Mairi regarded him heatedly in the kitchen. Her cheeks flushed with concern.

Hamish came out of the bedroom just then and looked up at Logan with heartbreak in his wide eyes. "You're leaving?"

Logan knelt down on one knee. "Only for a little while."

"How long will that be?" Hamish asked.

Logan swallowed uneasily. "I don't know, lad. But I *will* be back. I promise."

He tousled Hamish's hair, then stood and faced Mairi. Her brow was knitted with apprehension and her expression mirrored her son's disappointment.

"I'm sorry, Mairi, but I must go. Do you understand?"

"Of course," she replied, though she spoke with her eyes directed at the floor. "He's your brother and this morning you thought he was dead, but now you have learned that he is alive and in danger. I could never expect you to remain here, doing nothing. Of course you must go."

"But you're not happy about it," Logan softly said, watching her turn away from him, untie her apron, and walk into their bedroom.

He followed her in and took hold of her arm.

Mairi shook her head. "It doesn't matter how I feel. You must go and search for your brother. There is no avoiding it."

"It *does* matter how you feel, Mairi, and I *will* come back. I swear it."

Her eyes lifted and he saw uncertainty in them. "Will you, truly?"

"Aye. You're my wife and I love you."

Her expression grew somber. "I know you do, and I love you, too, but you're about to ride out of here to try and raise an army and invade an English garrison. It's a perilous situation, Logan. I'm frightened that something will happen to you, and I don't want to lose you."

"I'll be careful," he said.

She let out a resigned sigh. "Then you must take my father's sword. You cannot leave here unarmed."

"I will bring it back to you," he said while she retrieved it, along with her father's sword belt, from on top of her wardrobe.

Logan's work around the croft had strengthened his arm considerably and he was confident the break would continue to heal as he buckled it around his waist.

"Is there nothing I can say to convince you not to go?" Mairi asked when their eyes met.

Recognizing her distress, Logan pulled her into his arms and held her tight. "You know me, lass. I'm reckless and passionate. I cannot possibly sit still, on my hands, doing nothing."

She drew away to look up at him. "I know, but I thought there was a chance you were ready to let go of that side of yourself. I thought you might be happy living in peace." She shook her head. "I was a fool to think I could change you."

He held her away from him at arms' length. "But you *have* changed me, Mairi. You've helped me face my shame, head on. I don't know what will become of me when I speak to Angus, but at least he will know who I really am and I will no longer be living a lie."

He lowered his mouth to hers and devoured her with his kiss. She responded with a desperate embrace, running her hands through his hair and clinging to his shoulders, squeezing his tartan in her fists.

"If you don't come back," she said breathlessly, "I will never forgive you."

He forced himself to let go of her, then backed away to begin preparations for their departure. "If I don't come back, lass, I'd have to be a dead man, because that's the only thing that could keep me from your bed."

He walked out and heard her say quietly behind him, "That's what I'm afraid of."

CHAPTER

FIFTEEN

For three days straight, Tomas and Logan road hard across
the lush green Highlands on their quest to reach Kinloch
Castle and make their plea to Angus the Lion. They were
but half a day's ride from the castle gates when they stopped
near a shallow burn in the forest to rest the horses and camp
for the night.

As Logan sat before the dying fire sipping strong wine and
feeling the chill of the late summer night, he pondered the circumstances in which he now found himself. Not long ago, he
had been content with a warrior's life, scouting these familiar
forests and glens with his brother Darach, day after day, week
after week, month after month.

Tonight, he was a married man, longing overwhelmingly
for the pleasure of his wife's touch, her smile, and the mouthwa-
tering aromas of her cooking at the end of the day.

At the same time, he was not sorry to be sitting outdoors
before a sputtering fire with Tomas Campbell, who had spent
the past three days regaling Logan with tales about his former
chief—Logan's own father—during the last years of his life.
Tomas and Logan's father had been as close as brothers and
Logan felt good—for the first time in his adult life—that someone other than his own brother Darach knew his true heritage.
The connection was fulfilling in a way he could not possibly
describe.

As a result, Logan let down his guard that night as he refilled his wine cup and drank thirstily. He shared his own stories with Tomas—details about what had occurred between him and Darach on the road to Leathan and how they had disagreed about what to do with Larena—which was how Logan had ended up with a broken arm. Tomas understood his desire for vengeance. He even admired him for it.

It was very late when Logan fell asleep, wrapped in his tartan, oblivious to the chill in the air.

When he woke at a wicked, ungodly hour, it was to see Tomas marching back into the camp with his hands clasped behind his head and a musket jabbing him in the back.

⋘⋙

"Logan, tell them who I am," Tomas shouted as he was shoved forward across a patch of ferns on the forest floor.

Still half asleep and cursing the effects of the wine from the night before, Logan sat up lazily and squinted at the two men who held the weapons. They were Scots, not Redcoats, and they wore the MacDonald tartan.

"Logan! Ye lazy arse!" Gawyn shouted with merriment. "Where the devil have ye been all this time? And what are ye doing, making camp with a Campbell?"

Both weapons were immediately lowered, and Logan grimaced against the pounding agony in his skull. "His name is Tomas and he's a friend. *Jesus*, Fergus!" He waved a hand in front of his nose. "When was the last time you took a bath?"

Fergus laughed, turned around and lifted his kilt to expose his bare, hairy bottom. "Missed me, did ya?"

Logan shielded his eyes. "Nay, I did not!"

He was vaguely aware of Tomas lowering his hands from behind his head and rolling his neck and shoulders, as if he were working hard to bury the urge to punch Fergus in the face.

"Tell us more," Gawyn said, plunking himself down next to Logan and rifling through his saddle bag, no doubt searching for something good to eat. "What have ye been up to? Angus thought ye were sleeping with the crows."

"I broke my arm," Logan explained. "I've been laying low, waiting for it to heal."

Fergus gestured toward Tomas, who stood in silence, observing their conversation. "Is that how you met this old bugger?"

"Aye," Logan replied, not quite ready to reveal *all* the particulars of the situation—namely, that he'd married the Campbell lass who'd found him in her field and given him care. "Like I said, he's a friend. We're on our way to Kinloch to speak to Angus."

"You don't need to travel all the way to Kinloch Castle for that," Gawyn told him.

Just then, a massive, pale gray warhorse emerged from the thick foliage, carrying none other than Angus the Lion himself.

Logan leapt quickly to his feet.

"Will wonders never cease," Angus said in a low, sinister voice as he dismounted and landed with a thud on the soft ground. His golden mane of hair fell forward, but he tossed it back with a flick of his head. "I didn't expect to ever lay eyes on you again, Logan. Not after you defied my orders and left your brother to finish your mission alone. I ought to thrash you senseless. God knows you deserve it." He strode away from his horse and approached the campsite. "Introduce me to your friend. Tomas Campbell, is it?"

"Aye," Tomas replied in his deep, guttural voice while his cheeks flushed red.

It was the first time Logan had seen Tomas appear intimidated, but Angus had that effect on most people. With his wintry blue eyes, an incomparable self-confidence and imposing muscular stature—not to mention his notorious reputation as a seasoned, ruthless warrior—he was a menacing presence to be sure.

Angus held out a hand. Tomas shook it.

"You've been recovering from a broken bone all this time?" Angus inquired of Logan. "You didn't feel it might be a wise idea to send word back to Kinloch? To let us know that you weren't lying dead in an English prison somewhere?"

Logan bowed his head and shook it. "Apologies, my laird. Things got out of hand. Darach and I quarreled. I was distracted."

"*Distracted*?" Logan felt the thrust of Angus's displeasure vibrate into the core of his chest. Angus narrowed his gaze. A muscle flicked at his jaw. "Walk with me."

Without waiting for Logan to speak, Angus shouldered his way past Tomas, and led Logan—alone—into the woods.

CHAPTER

SIXTEEN

⤚✦⤚

They walked a fair distance from the camp before Angus stopped and turned. "Tell me where you've been. What had you so distracted?"

While most men would probably consider Logan a fool for speaking so boldly to the great Lion, he couldn't help himself. He craved information. He had ridden halfway across the Highlands to glean it.

"First, will you tell me what you know of Darach? I thought he was dead, but then I was told he came here."

"Aye, he came," Angus replied without hesitation, "after raising the ire of the English by helping Fitzroy Campbell escape from prison. What a bloody circus *that* was. Did you know of it?"

Logan shook his head. "Not before it happened. I wasn't with Darach at the time, nor did I play a part in concocting that ludicrous plan, but I heard of it, after the fact. So he truly is alive then?"

"As far as I know. Although it's been over a week since I saw him last."

Logan could have collapsed to his knees with relief, but he managed to stay on his feet. "Where is he, Angus? Is he safe? And what about the Campbell lass, Larena? Is she alive as well?"

Angus gave Logan an ominous look of warning. "You're asking me questions when you've neglected to answer mine, Logan. Where were you all this time? Why did you not return?"

Logan exhaled sharply with a pang of apprehension, knowing there could be no avoiding Angus's interrogation. "I've been in Campbell territory, waiting for my arm to heal."

"An arm that was snapped by your brother, because the two of you had a disagreement on the road to Leathan. Am I right?"

Logan nodded. "Darach must have told you."

Angus circled around him like an ill-tempered shark. "Aye, he told me all about it. He said it had something to do with Larena, who you were supposed to deliver to Leathen, along with the King's pardon to save her father's life. She was also pledged to marry Colonel Gregory Chatham. Did you fancy her, Logan? Is that why Darach was forced to put you in your place?"

Logan glanced up with anger. "Nay, I did not fancy that woman. I had *other* desires. I wanted to use her to gain entry into the castle, then I wanted to kill her father myself." Realizing that he'd said too much, too quickly, Logan took a breath to try and cool the fires of rage that erupted in his blood at the mere memory of it. "Darach was against that plan."

"And rightly so," Angus said. "But tell me this. Her father was already sentenced to die. If you wanted him dead, you could have simply destroyed the pardon. Accidentally dropped it into a river while making your way across. Wouldn't that have been simpler?"

"I wanted to be the one to do it myself," Logan explained. "I wanted Fitzroy Campbell to look me in the eye and know exactly who was strangling the life out of him."

Angus's ice-blue eyes narrowed. He regarded Logan for a long moment, as if he already knew far too much about the situation. "Why?"

Logan swallowed uneasily while Angus continued to circle around him. "It's a long story," Logan replied. "It goes way back…fifteen years ago, to the Battle of Sheriffmuir."

Knowing that he could not possibly avoid telling the truth at this point, Logan suspected he and Angus might be here a while.

Angus raised an eyebrow. "Let me guess. You fled the battlefield with your brother and changed your names from Campbell to MacDonald."

Logan's head drew back in surprise. "You *knew*?"

Angus rolled his eyes heavenward, as if this were a dull and tedious affair.

"Yet you took us in, regardless?" Logan pressed.

Angus wagged a finger at him. "Make no mistake about it, lad. It was my father who took you in, not me. I doubt I would have been so forgiving. But I suspect it wasn't his benevolent nature or sympathetic heart that moved him to accept your oath of allegiance, because Lord knows he was a merciless brute at the best of times. I always thought he intended to use you as pawns against the Campbells somehow, eventually, since you were the chief's only surviving heirs. I don't know what his plan might have been, but that day never came to pass."

"He always treated us like sons," Logan said, with dismay.

Angus waved a hand through the air with bitter hostility. "Aren't you the lucky one? I, on the other hand, was his eldest, yet he told me repeatedly that I was a constant disappointment to him. But that's another story for another day. What are your intentions? You've come here with Tomas Campbell to speak to me. Do you have plans to seize your castle back from that slapdash English bully, Gregory Chatham?"

Logan shook his head as if to clear it. "You know about that plan, too?"

Angus's broad shoulders rose and fell with a sigh of impatience. "Shouldn't it be *Darach* leading that charge? He is your elder brother, is he not?"

"But he is *not here*," Logan reminded Angus firmly, with a shooting glare. "And I don't know where the devil he is. You have yet to tell me."

"That's right," Angus shouted in a deep and booming voice, striding forward aggressively and causing Logan to back up against a large oak. "I haven't told you a bloody thing, lad, because I owe you nothing. Darach, however..." Angus took a deep breath and calmed himself. "That's different. He saved my son's life, and for that, I owe him everything."

Logan turned around and rested his hand upon the gnarled trunk. "You still haven't revealed where he is."

Angus spoke in a cool voice. "I haven't, because I ought to be stringing you up by the ankles for disobeying my orders. It's only because I know how much Darach cares for you that I am restraining myself."

Logan faced him and gripped the handle of his sword, just in case Angus changed his mind and found himself in a mood to strike out.

"I always respected your brother," Angus continued, "but you were a reckless, impatient young misfit of a warrior. You never knew how to keep calm and wait for the dust to settle."

Logan nodded. "I'm aware of that flaw in my character, Angus, but I'm working to remedy it. And if you wish to know where I was all this time, I was being nursed back to health by a kind-hearted, bonnie lass in a crofter's cottage."

Angus inclined his head with understanding. "Ah."

"Her name is Mairi Campbell, and I took her as my wife."

"Your wife!" Angus scoffed, but there was a hint of a chuckle in it. "There it is again—the unbelievable impatience! She must have been a very bonnie lass indeed, if you wanted to shag her badly enough to walk down the aisle for her."

"It wasn't like that," Logan tried to explain. He turned away again. "You wouldn't understand."

No one could *ever* understand how Mairi had burrowed her way into the depths of his soul and calmed the storm of his hatred and desire for vengeance. She had shown him what it felt like to love and be loved. To feel gratitude instead of pessimism and anger.

And yet, as he gripped her father's sword in a tight fist, he did not feel ready to give up the warrior side of himself. He wasn't sure he would ever be able to do that.

"A woman can have an extraordinary effect on a man," Angus said thoughtfully. "I once believed a woman made a man weak, but it depends on the woman, I suppose. Some have the opposite effect."

Logan watched Angus stride about the clearing, tossing his knife into the air and catching it by the handle.

"Will you please tell me where Darach is?" Logan finally asked.

Angus strode closer and spoke softly. "The fact is, I don't know. A month ago, I sent him to seek sanctuary with the Duke of Moncrieffe. He hid in the whisky distillery for a time, but a week ago, he and Larena boarded a ship for France under assumed names. I cannot tell you any more than that. I don't know where they landed or if they will ever return."

Logan closed his eyes as a bitter cold despair washed over him. "Darach left the country?"

That meant he might not ever see his brother again, much less reach a reconciliation over their differences.

"He did," Angus said. "And he was worried about you, Logan. No one knew where you were—if you were dead or alive. You should have sent word."

Logan cupped his forehead in his hand. "I know that now. But here we are and that cannot be changed." He looked up.

Angus regarded him shrewdly. "Aye, here we are. You, with an axe to grind, arriving at my gates with the former Laird of War from Leathan Castle, while a vindictive English tyrant is wreaking havoc up and down the glens of Scotland. It reminds me of something that happened a while back."

"What is that?" Logan asked with a curious frown.

Angus gave him a look. "That is yet another story for another day. But I will say this: Colonel Gregory Chatham is not the first English officer we've had to…" He paused. "*Restrain.* And you're not the first out-of-control Highlander with an axe to grind."

"I'm not out of control," Logan assured him. "Not any-more. But I've heard what Chatham has been doing. I cannot allow him to continue on his warpath."

"I'm pleased to hear it," Angus said. "I am of the same mind. Chatham must be stopped. One way or another."

"What do you have in mind?" Logan asked, strolling closer with interest.

"All sorts of things, but most importantly, it begins with the Campbell clan reclaiming their castle."

"But they've all scattered," Logan said. "They have no chief and the English army won't take kindly to a requests that they hand their garrison back to the Scots."

"I am hardly imagining a *friendly* request," Angus explained. "Seizing the castle will take strength and numbers. To achieve that, you Campbells have no choice but to form an alliance."

"With the MacDonalds?" Logan asked, raising his eyebrows in disbelief that the suggestion of an alliance would come from Angus.

"Only temporarily," Angus replied with a glimmer of dark purpose in his eyes—and a hint of amusement. "Until we rid the Highlands of Colonel Gregory Chatham. Then we can go back to hating each other."

Logan looked away, toward the camp. "Tomas was my father's laird of war. He should be here for this discussion."

"Aye," Angus replied. "And if we're going to work together, I'll need him to return to Campbell territory as quickly as possible and raise an army. My men can be ready to move at a moment's notice. We can combine our forces near Leathan."

Logan strode closer and spoke with amazement. "You're prepared to do that, Angus? To lead your army to help the Campbells reclaim their castle?"

Angus's eyes narrowed as he laid a hand on Logan's shoulder. "Nay, *I'm* not going to lead them, Logan. *You* are."

Logan stared, speechless, while shock wedged in his throat.

"You would be willing to put the Kinloch army into *my* hands?" Logan asked. "I'm a deserter, Angus, not to mention a Campbell, and I've been lying to you for fifteen years."

Angus nodded. "Aye, but you've never deserted *me*, nor are you lying to me now. I cannot think of a more skilled warrior, nor anyone else more motivated to break down those gates, toss the Redcoats out onto their dirty arses, and take back the home you've always longed for."

"Angus…"

His chief cut him off. "Every man deserves a chance at redemption, Logan. I know that better than anyone, as I've made my own mistakes. You may be reckless and impatient, but you are no coward, and what we need is a fiery-tempered champion to rid this country of the likes of Gregory Chatham. In light of what he's been doing to my clansmen and women, I want him gone. Or stone-cold dead, lying at the bottom of a ravine somewhere. Either will do."

Logan couldn't help but savor the idea of sending Chatham back to England—or to hell.

Indeed…either would do.

"I won't disappoint you," Logan said.

Angus re-sheathed his knife. "Good. Now the first order of business is for us to discuss plans with Tomas Campbell. Then you and he will meet a family not far from here who was burned out by Colonel Chatham and his undisciplined company of Redcoats, who did far worse than burn their home and kill their livestock. The son is dead and the daughter was dragged into the woods. After meeting them, you will then take this news to the Duke of Moncrieffe. He won't give us an army—that much I know because he is a diplomat above all else—but we'll need his political support. He has the ear of the King and he may be able to evoke some sympathy for our side. He must know what is taking place."

"I can leave here today," Logan said, wanting nothing more than to meet the man who had given Darach sanctuary in his whisky distillery. Perhaps, as well as support them in their plans, the duke would know where Darach had gone.

CHAPTER

SEVENTEEN

~⋙~

It was typically a two-day ride from Kinloch Castle to Moncrieffe's ducal estate, but Logan was highly motivated and impelled by his characteristic furor and lack of patience. Not only did he crave information about Darach's whereabouts, but after meeting the family that had been treated appallingly and unforgivably—especially the young woman who had suffered in the worst possible way—he wanted nothing more than to rid this country of the likes of Colonel Chatham. To stop such atrocities from ever happening again. To drive the English out of the Campbell stronghold once and for all.

Beneath all of that, he wanted to return home to Mairi, assure her that he was safe and make love to her ardently and single-mindedly until he could no longer think, see, or breathe.

As he rode his horse across the Highlands, he wondered how in the world Mairi had succeeded in digging her way into his heart so deeply and thoroughly. He'd never imagined any woman could possess so much power over him, enough to smother the flames of his discontent and inspire a different sort of passion in him—a passion that left him burning with pure unmitigated desire to hold her in his arms again, smell the fragrance of her soft bare flesh in the deep of night, and bury himself in her heated, womanly depths.

Most of all, he wanted to keep her safe from any further harm.

Continuing over countless damp moors and across dangerous, fast-moving rivers, Logan imagined their reunion with longing and feverish intensity. He fell asleep at night under the stars with only one thought on his mind. *Mairi.*

It seemed that she had lit a fire of passion inside of him, yet it was strange that, when he was with her, simply working her farm or sitting at the water's edge talking, he felt a calm he'd never known before. It was the oddest combination of emotions—passion, obsession and a deep, long-awaited tranquility.

Was that not the perfect way to live? he asked himself over and over as he galloped thunderously into shady forests and across moonlit glens.

Yet, here he was, committed to a new mission—for his laird and for his clan. He had promised to fulfill a different duty outside his role as husband, which left him many miles from his wife's warm, inviting bed.

No doubt, she too was alone—longing desperately for him. He knew it because he was confident in her love. Even from many miles away, he felt it in his soul.

⌒⋞⋅⋟⌒

On the second day of Logan's journey to the duke's estate—late in the afternoon, when he was only a few miles from the gatehouse—he stopped on a pebbly beach at the edge of a loch. He did not know the name of that particular body of water, but it was an oasis that drew him out of the forest like some sort of magical beacon.

Exhausted and knowing that it would be ill-mannered to cross a duke's threshold smelling like an unwashed heathen, Logan walked his horse to where the waves lapped gently onto the shore, and dismounted.

"Drink up," he said to Tracker. "I'm thirsty, as well."

Kneeling down, he scooped some water into his hand and raised it to his lips.

A moment later, he was back on his feet, unbuckling his sword belt, removing his tartan, and stripping off his shirt. The boots came off next and he dropped everything in an untidy pile at the water's edge. A few seconds later, he waded into the loch, naked as the day he was born, then dove in.

Kersplash! The chilly water bombarded his senses and he broke the surface with a cry of shock. "*Sweet Jesus, Mary, and Joseph! That's cold!*"

Taking a few short breaths to calm his pounding heart, he swam further out, giving himself time to grow accustomed to the chill. Wishing he had soap, he made do by scrubbing at his scalp with the pads of his fingers and swimming under the water for extended periods of time.

That's when something caught his eye.

At the bottom of the loch—a flash of light on metal.

It reflected the rays of the sun that speared through the murky, undulating depths.

Rising to the surface to drink in as much air as he could, Logan treaded water for a moment, then dove straight down to the bottom where he finally placed his hands on what appeared to be a weapon.

A sword, still in its leather scabbard and belt. The tip was buried deep in the sand and he had to tug its considerable weight relentlessly through the resistance of the water.

A few seconds later he broke the surface again with the heavy claymore in his hand. He sucked in a massive breath of air, and swam back to shore.

Wading out of the loch and onto the pebbly beach—barely noticing the chill of the air on his nude body—he examined the exquisitely designed basket hilt of the sword and the large gemstone at the top. The stone was cream colored with veins of gray and specks of sparkling crystal.

Impressed by the detail of the workmanship—which appeared to be ancient—and the sheer size and weight of the claymore, he slowly slid it out of the wet scabbard and examined the blade.

Though in need of a polish, it was a fine sword indeed, the most impressive Logan had ever seen. He swung it through the air with his good arm, lunged forward to strike an imaginary death blow, and swung it again. *Ach*, it was a perfectly remarkable piece of weaponry!

Pausing and turning toward the water, he gazed in all directions, wondering who in their right mind would have discarded such a priceless treasure. He wondered who it had belonged to and how long it had been sitting at the bottom of the loch. How had it come to be there?

Logan shivered suddenly, and realized he needed to get dressed before he went numb and froze to death. Sliding the sword back into its leather case, he donned his shirt and tartan, pinned it at his shoulder with his brooch, then pulled on his boots and secured Mairi's father's sword to his saddlebags.

Crouching down, he picked up the heavy claymore he had found in the loch and fastened it with the wet belt around his hips.

It fit perfectly. The weight of it felt good on his body.

Aye, this was an excellent find. A priceless treasure, to be sure. Far too magnificent a weapon not to be worn by its finder.

EIGHTEEN

The sun was just setting when Logan emerged from the forest onto a lush green field. He reined in his horse, for there it was in the distance—the famed Castle Moncrieffe. Logan decided in that moment that whoever had decided to call it a castle was grossly understating the majesty of the estate, for the main structure looked more like a French palace.

It stood on a small grassy island, surrounded by stone walls and drum bastions that rose high up from the water. A drawbridge and gate tower provided protection from the mainland, along with outbuildings around an inner bailey. Behind the main house, a more ancient-looking keep could be reached by a bridge corridor over the water.

Kicking in his heels, Logan urged his mount onward and hurried to cross the field and reach the gatehouse before the sun went down.

When Logan was questioned by the guard at the gate, all he had to do was present his sealed letter of introduction from Angus the Lion, Laird of Kinloch. Immediately, he was admitted. He rode his horse across the bridge, beneath the raised iron portcullis, where Tracker was attended to by a groom, and Logan was escorted across the bailey to the main house.

A servant in a curly black wig and elegant livery greeted him at the door and invited him into the hall where they passed through a stone archway to a small, elegant reception room. The manservant instructed Logan to wait there, then he left him alone to look around and ponder the incomprehensible grandeur of his surroundings.

Though Kinloch Castle was an impressive Scottish citadel with an enormous banquet hall and luxurious bedchambers throughout, there was something rustic and medieval about the place. It was nothing compared to this ornate palace with marble columns, priceless paintings and sculptures, upholstered chairs and elegant draperies, and collections of colorful porcelain vases displayed inside glass cabinets.

The reception room was paneled in dark wood. On the wall, above the fireplace, hung an enormous portrait of a ferocious-looking warrior in an armored breastplate and kilt. Logan stared at the painting for a long while, reaching an understanding as to how this family had achieved such tremendous power and property over the centuries—no doubt through brutal battles and the ruthless spilling of blood. Logan strode closer to examine the threatening expression in the warlord's eyes...

"Good evening."

He jumped and turned at the sound of a low, yet reverberating voice from the open door. Logan found himself dumbstruck as he regarded the tall, brawny aristocrat dressed in a fine green brocade evening coat with extravagant lace cuffs and cravat, and a kilt of the MacLean tartan. His high black boots were polished to a fine sheen and his hair, dark with hints of gray at the temples, was tied back in a tidy queue.

Logan lowered his gaze and bowed, for he had never been presented to a duke before, nor any other gentleman of such high-ranking. "Your grace. It is an honor."

The duke strolled casually into the room and stopped in front of Logan, who looked up at last.

"The honor is mine, sir," the duke replied. "Angus MacDonald is a good friend. We go back many years. I read his letter just now. He speaks highly of you."

Logan hadn't actually read the letter of introduction, for it had been sealed. But he was relieved to hear that it mentioned nothing about desertion, or the fact that he had been living his life as an imposter since the day he set foot upon MacDonald territory at the age of eleven.

"And of course I met your brother, Darach," the duke continued. "He worked for me as a night watchman at my distillery. He was here for over a month."

Logan's heart began to pound with anticipation. "Aye, Angus mentioned that. Thank you for your kindness to my brother, your grace. But may I ask...?"

"Yes?"

Logan cleared his throat nervously. "Could you tell me where he has gone? We parted on rather ugly terms, and I do not wish to leave things as they were."

The duke spoke matter-of-factly. "I gave him my word that I would tell no one of his whereabouts."

Logan exhaled heavily. "I understand, but I wish to explain myself to him. To *apologize*."

The duke regarded Logan curiously for a moment, then at last he responded. "If you wish to pen a letter while you are here, I will see that it is delivered."

And that was the end of that. The duke crossed to the other side of the room, picked up the crystal whisky decanter from the side table and poured two glasses. He offered one to Logan.

"Much obliged." Logan sipped the splendid, first-class whisky and remembered how genuinely he had appreciated it on his first night in Mairi's stable, when it had helped to abate his physical agony. Tonight it was coming in handy to calm his nerves.

"Angus has written that there have been troubles with the English colonel in charge of the garrison at Leathan," the duke said. "Have you met Gregory Chatham?"

"Nay, your grace. I've only heard tell of him from others."

"Is there any chance that the stories are exaggerated?"

Logan swallowed back the bile that rose in his throat at the memory of what Angus had shown him the other day. "Nay, your grace. I saw for myself the evidence of Chatham's brutality. There was a family on MacDonald territory. Chatham ordered the house and stable to be burned with all the livestock inside. The son was killed and the daughter was used in the worst possible way."

A muscle twitched at the duke's jaw. "Is she alive?" he asked with an intense, fevered stare.

"Aye, but she said she *wished* she were dead."

The duke downed the full contents of his glass, turned his back on Logan and poured himself another. Logan listened to the sound of the liquid spilling into the glass.

"This feels familiar," the duke said in a quiet, gruff voice. "I once knew a British officer, many years ago, who was much like Chatham. He was courteous on the surface and behaved like a gentleman for the most part, but his heart was black as night." The duke faced Logan again and sipped his whisky. His lips pulled back, baring his teeth. "Not all British soldiers are bad. I've met some very good men—*honorable* men—over the years who I would welcome at my table any day. But others..." He drank again, then set down his glass and returned to the center of the room.

As he approached, his gaze fell to the claymore at Logan's hip. The duke stopped where he was, stared at it intensely, then frowned and lowered his voice to an almost imperceptible utterance. "Where did you get that sword?"

Logan felt a shakiness in all his limbs and extremities at the possibility that the sword belonged to the duke and he was about to accuse Logan of stealing it. His hand moved to grip the handle. "*This?*"

"Aye, that."

Clearing his throat, he began to explain. "I found it today." "Where?"

Logan swallowed uneasily. "I went for a swim, west of here. It was buried in the sand at the bottom of a loch. Do you recognize it, your grace? If it belongs to you and you wish to have it back..."

"*Nay,*" the duke barked. "You found it. It is yours. But I do recognize it." He strode closer and held out his hand. "May I?"

"Of course." Logan set down his glass, then slid the weapon out of its leather scabbard. He laid it flat on both his palms and offered it to the duke.

Moncrieffe picked it up, examined the blade, as well as the elaborately carved basket hilt and the Mull agate at the tip of the handle. After a moment, he turned away and swung it through the air a few times with the skills of a master swordsman.

At last, he faced Logan and handed it back. "A fine weapon indeed. Use it wisely, and well."

"Thank you." Logan accepted it and slid it back into its casing. "But you mentioned that you recognized it. May I enquire as to its owner?"

A brief flash of something almost diabolical danced across the duke's features. Then he backed up a few steps. "Aye. That is no ordinary sword, Logan. It once belonged to the Butcher of the Highlands."

Logan felt suddenly breathless. "The famous Scottish legend who slayed entire armies of Redcoats singlehandedly? Some say he was naught but a ghost. The ghost of a barbarian."

The corner of the duke's mouth curled up with touch of amusement. "I suspect he did have the blood of a barbarian running through his veins, but he was true flesh and blood. I know because I met him once. And he *was* barbaric."

Overcome with curiosity, Logan strode closer. "You *met* him? What ever became of him? They say he simply disappeared…vanished into thin air. I also heard that the English continue to hold his shield, which they keep at Fort William as a prize."

"I've heard that, too," the duke agreed. "So it's likely that the Butcher *is* dead, especially if you found his sword at the bottom of a loch. He was probably captured, killed, and tossed over a boat rail. Either way, he is a remnant of the past. Nothing now but an ancient piece of history."

Logan gripped the handle of the sword and gazed down at the gray-and-white gemstone on the handle. "Surely I am not worthy of this. Someone else should have it."

"Such as whom?" the duke asked, seeming genuinely dumbfounded.

"I don't know," Logan replied. "You? Or Angus the Lion? I am nobody."

Moncrieffe raised an eyebrow. "The Butcher was a nobody as well. And I am sure, if he were alive today, he would be more than pleased to learn it would be used to reclaim a Scottish castle that was seized by the English. Like I said, use it well."

In that moment, Logan experienced an exhilarating rush of sensation at the thought of charging through the gates of Leathan Castle, wielding the sword that once belonged to one of the most courageous and heroic Scottish warriors of all time.

Logan thought of his father dying at the hands of his enemy and the subsequent loss of the Campbell stronghold to the English.

Wouldn't his father be pleased to know that his death would be avenged, and his castle returned to his clan—as if the Butcher himself had risen from the grave to see it through? Perhaps this was Logan's true destiny after all—to become the warrior he'd always wanted to be, even as a boy when he was not yet ready to step onto a battlefield.

But he was ready now. He was more than ready.

His heart raced at the prospect of taking back the castle that had once been his birthright.

A passing image of Mairi flashed in his brain suddenly. He remembered how she had wanted him to stay with her. She had feared he would put himself in danger.

He cared for Mairi deeply and did not wish to cause her pain. She would most certainly be grief-stricken if he were killed during the invasion.

But if he survived and was successful in taking back the castle? What then? What about their quiet, peaceful life in the glen?

Picking up his whisky glass, he quickly finished it off.

The duke gestured for Logan to follow him, and Logan had to shake himself out of the flood of his confounding thoughts.

"Come with me now," the duke said. "I will have my butler show you to a room for the night, and my valet will get you some clean clothes—something appropriate for dinner. The duchess will enjoy making your acquaintance, as will my brother Iain, and his wife. After dinner, we will retire to the library for brandy to discuss your plan of attack. I'll offer advice and my brother is an excellent military strategist. You will learn much from him."

Logan followed Moncreiffe to the door.

"I will also send word to the King," the duke continued, "as well as Lord Rutherford, who is Gregory Chatham's father. They must both be made aware of what that foolish lad is up to, for it will jeopardize English and Scottish relations if he continues to harass the Highlanders. I know for a fact that the King wishes to avoid another uprising."

"I believe we all wish that," Logan agreed as he followed the duke into the main hall. "Most of us do, at any rate."

The duke gave him a shrewd look of agreement.

⋘⋈⋙

The following morning at dawn—after a late night with the duke and his brother where he learned much about English military strategy, then later, penned a long, personal letter to Darach—Logan mounted his horse to return to Kinloch and make preparations for the march on Leathan Castle.

As he kicked in his heels and galloped out of the bailey and across the bridge, every fragment of his body hummed with anticipation for the battle ahead. He imagined the moment he would behold the interior of Leathan Castle for the first time in many years. Would everything look the same? Would he be able to recall where his bedchamber was located? Would he sleep there again if the invasion was a success?

As it stood now, the clan was without a chief, the castle had no laird, and leadership would have to fall to someone. Perhaps the clan would desire Tomas in that position. He was, after all, a loyal Campbell and a brilliant, courageous warrior—a good man with a heart of honor. He had also been the one to push Logan to secure an alliance between the MacDonalds and Campbells to help reclaim their castle. None of this would be happening if not for Tomas.

Yet, a part of Logan felt as if the lairdship should belong to his brother, Darach. And if not him, to no one other than himself—for he and his brother were the true blood heirs of Ronald James Campbell. Could it be that this was some sort of divine providence?

Ach...maybe it was only the Butcher's sword and the dazzle of the rising sun that was filling Logan with superstitious dreams of destiny and magic. Even the notion that a ghost warrior might inhabit his body on the day of the battle...

Logan felt almost invincible as he rode into the woods, imagining the attack on Leathan Castle, for he had one slick trick up his sleeve—a trick that would put the English at a severe disadvantage, undeniably.

It was not until Logan reached the loch where he'd found the Butcher's sword that he realized he had not thought of Mairi once since he woke that morning, mounted his horse, and galloped away from Moncrieffe Castle.

Normally, Mairi was the first thing on his mind each day—her smile, her sweet fragrance, the pleasure of her touch—but his conversations with the duke the night before still occupied every corner of his mind. There was no room for anything in his brain but designs of warfare.

The realization caused a sharp stab of heartache in his chest, for he knew now what lay ahead of him. Long before he'd met Mairi, he had dreamed of vengeance and atonement, but now it was so much greater than that. It was not simply his own selfish desires for revenge and redemption that drove him. It was a need to fix all that was broken within the Campbell clan, and rid Leathan Castle—and the whole of Scotland—of a tyrant.

Today, there was no room in his heart for a woman. Today, Logan was a warrior, and right or wrong, he was compelled to fight for an elevated cause.

Nineteen

Mairi stood in the open door of the stable at dawn, her breath catching in her throat.

An English Redcoat, with two eggs in his hand, stood over one of her chickens. He jumped at the sight of her, dropped the eggs on the ground with a splat, and drew his pistol. "Stay where you are. Hands in the air."

A burst of white-hot fear exploded in her belly. Heart racing, she raised her hands over her head. "Take what you need and leave," she said to him. "We want no trouble here."

Keeping the weapon trained on her face, he squinted at her with suspicion. "Who are *we*? How many men are in the house?"

"None," she replied. "It's only my mother, myself, and my son. He is just a wee lad."

"No men?" the soldier pressed. "I find that difficult to believe. Are you lying to me?"

Mairi shook her head. "Nay, I give you my word. It's just the three of us here. Now please take what you need, and leave."

He glanced down at the yellow egg yolk splattered on the toe of his boot. "Bloody hell." Then his eyes darted upward, as if he suddenly realized his mistake in taking his eyes off her.

She still stood in the doorway with her hands in the air.

The soldier removed the empty white sack from over his shoulder and held it out to her. "Fill this with eggs."

Cautiously, she moved closer to take the sack from him, and collected every last egg while he pointed his pistol at her. When there were no more eggs in the nests, she turned and handed the sack back to him.

Without reaching for it, he looked her up and down from head to foot, his gaze settling on her breasts for an uncomfortable stretch of time. "You say there are no men here. Where is your husband?"

A sick, angry feeling crept into her belly, for she recognized the softening tones of his voice and the obvious trail of his thoughts. "My husband traveled to Kinloch on an errand. He will return at any time. I expect him this morning."

It was a lie, of course. But she would say anything to protect herself.

"Kinloch, you say…" The soldier tilted his head to the side. "What's his name?"

She hesitated, wishing she'd kept Logan's destination to herself.

"I don't see how that is any of your business, sir."

He raised the pistol higher. "I'm a soldier in the King's army and *everything* in Scotland is my business." He paused and raised a dark, arched eyebrow at her. "If I want it to be."

Again, his leering gaze roamed presumptuously down the length of her body. She shivered with revulsion.

"Take the eggs and go," she demanded, pushing the bag at him. "There is nothing else here for you."

This time he took the sack of eggs from her and fastened it over his shoulder. "I'll be the one to decide whether or not there's anything here for me."

Mairi's heart hammered wildly as she backed away from him.

"Take me to the house. I want to see for myself that there are no men here."

"Why?"

"Because we're searching for someone," he explained. "A Scottish rebel who helped a prisoner escape from the garrison. His name is Darach MacDonald, though he may be going by the name of Campbell. Do you know him?"

Oh God...

"Nay, I do not."

He studied her expression for a long, heated moment, then grabbed her by the arm and dragged her roughly out of the stable. "Show me the house."

"Why?" she asked, stumbling as he shoved her.

He pressed the barrel of the pistol into her ribs. "We've been searching every house on our way to the garrison. I want to make sure you're not harboring a fugitive."

Mairi had no choice but to do as he commanded, for she didn't doubt that he would shoot her on the spot if she resisted him.

Seconds later, she pushed through the front door and showed him the empty kitchen. "See? There is no one here."

The soldier's angry gaze darted about the interior. "Show me all the beds."

"But my son is—"

"I don't care about your son. Show me." He glared at her with malice, and she worried that he might have more on his mind than the search for a fugitive.

She pointed at the door to her room. "Through there."

He gestured with the pistol. "Lead the way. I'll follow."

Reluctantly, she moved across the kitchen and pulled the curtain aside to reveal her bed. "You see? It's empty."

The soldier pushed by her to search every corner.

Just then, Hamish shuffled out of her mother's bedroom on the opposite side of the cottage. He rubbed his eye with his knuckle. "Ma? What's going on?"

"Nothing, Hamish. Go back to bed."

The soldier hurried by her to see Hamish for himself. "This is your son?"

Hamish's eyes grew wide as saucers as he peered up at the soldier's intimidating red uniform and the pistol in his hand. He turned and bolted back into Isla's room.

"You frightened him," Mairi said with displeasure.

The soldier quickly followed Hamish. His boots pounded heavily across the floor and he disappeared behind the curtain. Mairi darted forward to stop him just as there was a scuffle and a clattering sound—as if the pistol had been knocked to the floor. The solider backed out of the room and returned to the kitchen with his hands in the air.

"It's time for you to leave now," Isla said, striding forward with her own pistol aimed at his face. Hamish remained in the bedroom.

"Fine," he said. "But if I find out that you know anything about that rebel Scot, there'll be hell to pay."

Isla escorted the soldier to the door. "Mairi, go and get his pistol on the floor in my room. Empty the chamber and return it to him."

Mairi hurried to complete the task. A moment later, they watched from the window as the Redcoat made his way across their back field and disappeared into the forest.

Mairi let out a breath of relief and sank down onto a chair. "That was close. I'm glad he was alone."

"We might not be so lucky next time," Isla replied as she sat down at the table across from Mairi.

"This sort of thing has been happening more and more lately," Mairi said. "Ever since the English took control of Leathan. They're everywhere, always coming around. I don't feel safe anymore."

"Nor do I," Isla replied. "At least that dirty Redcoat left without putting up a fight." She set the pistol down on the table and regarded Mairi intently, and lowered her voice so that Hamish would not hear. "Let me ask you something. What would you have done if he had turned out to be Joseph Kearney? Would you have dirked him in the back before you allowed him to walk through that door? Or would you have let him go off with our eggs?"

Mairi felt a rush of annoyance at being asked such a question. "I don't know what I would have done. If he had agreed to leave peacefully..." She stood up and went to light the fire for breakfast.

"Then what?" Isla asked. "You would have let him leave without paying a price for what he did to you five years ago?"

Crouching down on her knees at the hearth, Mairi glanced over her shoulder at her mother. "Now you're starting to sound like Logan."

"And what's wrong with that? I'm sure if Logan were here and Joseph Kearney tried to set foot in your bedroom, he would have stopped him from breathing, right then and there."

Mairi set the kindling in place and struck the flint. "I don't know why we're even talking about this. That soldier was not Captain Kearney, and you know very well that I've given up thoughts like those. I choose peace and forgiveness, not fear and hate, because I cannot live like that."

Isla let out a frustrated breath. "You may find, one of these days, that you have no choice but to muster up a great deal of fear and hatred in order to protect yourself and your son."

"If that day comes," Mairi replied, "I will do what I must to protect Hamish, but until then, let us speak no more of it. That soldier left without causing any real damage, and I am glad, because I don't want to kill anyone."

Isla raised an eyebrow knowingly. "And yet you always keep that knife hidden in your boot. You slide it into place each and every morning."

Mairi gave her mother a warning look. "All that soldier wanted was eggs. We're fine. It's over. I don't want to talk about it anymore."

With that, she walked out of the kitchen to go and see if one of the hens might have laid a late egg or two.

⚜

Sitting back in the chair in his tent, Colonel Gregory Chatham turned his cheek to the side so that his manservant could run the razor under his jawline. All the while, Gregory tapped his finger persistently on the armrest, for he was growing more irritable with every passing second. "Hurry up, Fenwick. I don't have all day."

He had been living out of a tent for weeks, sitting in a saddle from sunup to sundown, and he was weary of the outdoors, not to mention his grating frustration—for he still hadn't found that rebel bastard, Darach Campbell. Or Larena.

At this point, Gregory had no further interest in taking her as his wife. That ship had sailed. He wouldn't take her back now if she got down on her knees, kissed his boots, cried a river of tears, and pleaded hysterically. Although he would certainly enjoy seeing that.

What he *really* wanted was to kill them both. First, he would drive a dull, rusty blade through Darach's belly—in return for the humiliation he'd caused Gregory by escaping a second time. Gregory would force Larena to watch Darach die slowly and painfully. Then Gregory would wrap a rope around her neck and strangle the life out of her.

He thought carefully about that for a few seconds. Larena would probably faint before she actually expired...

Would that be satisfying at all? He supposed it would be fitting at least—a far more decorous end for such a beautiful woman.

A knock sounded at the entrance to his tent just then and hauled him from his daydreams. "Come in!"

Captain Joseph Kearney bent under the tent flap. "Good morning, Colonel. I thought you might like to know that Lieutenant Johnson just returned with some eggs that are being prepared now. He found them in a crofter's stable about a half a mile from here."

Gregory waved his servant away and sat forward. "Did he search the premises?"

"Yes, sir. He said there were no men, just a Scotswoman, her young son, and her mother. He did enquire after the rebel, but the women knew nothing."

"That's it?" Gregory asked with a frown. "I thought you were going to tell me that she'd seen something, or heard something."

"No, sir."

Gregory's stomach turned over with sickening dread, for he was not looking forward to writing the report of his failure to his father in Edinburgh. How could he possibly explain that he had tracked Darach Campbell all the way to Kinloch Castle, had him on the floor at the tip of his sword, but was outdone at the last second and had no choice but to let him go? It would not be

a pleasant letter to write. Gregory should have killed the lieutenant who had witnessed it, but it was too late now. Others knew.

With soap dripping from his chin, Gregory stood. "Thank
you, Captain. Go get yourself some breakfast."

The man turned to go, but hesitated. "If you like, Colonel,
I could go now and question the women myself. Sometimes a
firmer hand will get different results."

Gregory regarded Kearney with displeasure and hostility. "I know exactly what your intentions are, Captain, and
there comes a time when your 'activities' in the name of the
King smack of self-indulgence. You've had your fill of Scottish
women over the past fortnight—and I've allowed it because
some degree of sport within the ranks is good for morale—yet
I have seen nothing to suggest that your 'firm hand' will bring
me the rebel I am searching for. We do not have time to wait
while you skip off to satisfy your depravity. This is the British
Army, not a brothel, and we must get back to the garrison."

Captain Kearney gave him a devious look. "It wouldn't
take long, sir. I'd catch up."

This was a flagrant display of disrespect—which was all
Darach Campbell's fault for making Gregory appear weak in
front of his men.

"No!" he shouted at Captain Kearney. "I gave you a direct
order, sir—to go and get your breakfast. You will remain here and
prepare for our departure." He waved his manservant back to continue shaving him. "God, I'm sick of this wretched place. I once
had romantic notions about Scotland. Now I see that in actuality,
it is hell on earth and even turns *Englishmen* into savages."

Captain Kearney stalked out of Gregory's tent, while the
razor scraped noisily up the length of Gregory's throat.

CHAPTER

Twenty

Logan galloped his horse across the wooden bridge at Kinloch Castle, entered the bailey, and dismounted. While Tracker was attended to by a groom, Logan was escorted up the east tower steps to the sunlit solar where Angus—along with his cousin and Laird of War, Lachlan MacDonald—awaited his arrival.

"Welcome back," Angus said, greeting Logan with a firm handshake. Logan shook hands with Lachlan as well, while Angus turned to the drinks tray on the sideboard beneath the tapestry on the far wall.

"You must tell us of your meeting with Moncrieffe," Angus said. "Was he keen to send word to the King about what has been happening here? Did he agree with your plan to invade Leathan?"

Angus approached Logan and Lachlan with two glasses of whisky. Logan accepted his gratefully. "Aye, the duke is an extraordinary man. I feel blessed to have shared a table with him. The duchess was lovely as well," Logan mentioned. "Despite being English."

Angus clinked glasses with Logan. "Indeed. Now tell me. Lachlan and I both wish to know. What is your plan? What advice did Moncrieffe give you?"

Logan sipped his drink and took a moment to appreciate its fine essence. "He and his brother Iain shared their knowledge of English military strategy. But one thing in particular kept repeating itself."

"What was that?" Lachlan asked with a tilt of his head, for he, too, was a brilliant military strategist and seasoned warrior.

"I believe the duke has some unique experience with battles of a lesser degree," Logan replied.

Angus paused. "You are referring to hand-to-hand combat. Smaller, well-timed skirmishes?"

"Aye, and the element of surprise," Logan added.

Angus and Lachlan shared a knowing look. "A tool that should never be squandered."

Logan raised his glass. "Indeed. And I believe, if we are to succeed in taking back Leathan Castle, we must use every means at our disposal. You are trusting me with your army, Angus, despite the fact that I am a Campbell by blood. For that trust, I am grateful. In return, I will trust you both with a Campbell secret and my strategy for the invasion. If I tell you this, will you give me your word of honor that you will never use it against us in years to come?"

In that moment, Angus glanced down at the ancient sword Logan carried at his hip. He stared at it for a long moment, then met Logan's gaze. "Are you about to astonish me? Because I have a sneaking suspicion you know something splendid."

"I do," Logan replied with a smile. "And though I know how much you love to use your battering ram, we may not need it."

Angus's blue eyes narrowed enquiringly. "I am intrigued." He gestured for Logan to walk with him and Lachlan to the windows, where they could look out at the rolling hills and forests, and discuss the plan of attack.

◈

At the sound of approaching hooves across her back field, Mairi's eyes lifted from her stitching. She and Isla exchanged looks of concern.

"Who could it be at this hour?" Mairi asked in a quiet voice, not wanting to wake Hamish, who had just fallen asleep. "It's after dark."

Setting aside the stocking she had just begun to mend—and praying it was not another British soldier coming to steal from them, or do worse—she rose from her chair in front of the fire and crossed to the window to look out.

It was a damp, foggy night. She could see nothing through the blackness beyond the glass.

She heard the rider enter the yard and dismount. Isla reached for the pistol she kept by her chair and cocked the hammer, while Mairi moved stealthily, with a pounding heart, to answer the door.

The intruder knocked softly, and Mairi's fear turned instantly to joy, for she knew that was not the knock of a Redcoat. The man at the door was someone who did not wish to wake Hamish after bedtime.

Flinging the door open, she stared wide-eyed at Logan. As soon as their eyes met, he smiled. He was so handsome, every bone in her body turned to mush. Her heart leapt and she threw herself into his arms.

"Ah, my darling lass," he whispered in her ear, nuzzling her neck and holding her close. "You have no idea how I've missed you."

"I've missed you, too," she replied, pressing her cheek against the rock-hard wall of his chest, breathing in the intoxicating aromas of leather, horse, and the briny scent of the outdoors.

She was unaware of her mother rising from her chair and sneaking off to bed. Mairi only realized it when she dragged Logan inside the house and turned around, expecting to see Isla rising from her chair to greet him as well.

But Isla was gone. The kitchen was empty and quiet, except for the crackling fire in the hearth.

"It is so good to see you," Mairi whispered, facing him again. "Are you hungry? Can I fix you something to eat?"

He shook his head. "I'm only hungry for the sight of *you*, lass."

It was a lovely compliment, but she felt a stirring of unease as he continued to stand just inside the doorway, as if he were a guest there, not the husband who had shared her bed for weeks.

"Please, come in," she urged, reaching for his hand and tugging him forward, leading him closer to the fire. "Tell me about your journey. Or better yet, hold me, Logan. I don't think I can survive another day without the warmth of your body next to mine."

He joined her in front of the fire where she wrapped her arms around his waist, rested her cheek against his chest again. This time, however, he reached around, unfastened her clasped hands behind his back, and gently pushed her away. "I'm sorry, lass...I cannot stay."

She gazed up at him and frowned. "Why not? It's past nightfall. Where must you go at this hour?"

Logan continued to back away from her. Her stomach clenched tight with apprehension and dread for she knew in that moment that he had not truly come home to her. Nor did he have any intention of making love to her. Not tonight.

"I only came because I thought you deserved to know what is taking place."

"And what is that?" she asked, feeling rejected by his unexpected response to her touch.

Logan inhaled deeply. "There will be a battle at Leathan Castle in a few days' time, and I will be leading the Kinloch army through the gates."

"The *Kinloch* army..." Mairi frowned. "But they are MacDonalds and we are Campbells. What are your intentions, Logan? To seize the castle for Angus the Lion? Does Tomas know of this?"

"Of course he knows," Logan replied. "The alliance was his idea, remember? And he is raising a Campbell army as we speak. We will join forces a few miles from Leathan and drive the English out together. In the meantime, the Duke of Moncrieffe has sent word to the King to inform him of what is transpiring. He will plead for our cause—and the duke is certain that the King will be pleased to know it has nothing to do with the Jacobite uprisings. All we want is freedom from the atrocities that have been taking place under the leadership of Colonel Gregory Chatham. He has proved himself to be a madman, lass, and if the King wants to keep the peace with Scotland, he will listen to the duke, give the Campbells back their castle, and remove Chatham from his commission here in the Highlands."

Mairi labored to listen to all of this with an open, objective mind. "Are you certain the duke will help us? How can you be sure?"

"I am sure," Logan explained, "because I met him. I dined with him ten days ago."

Mairi had thought she'd heard it all since Logan walked through the door, but this caused her eyebrows to fly up. "You *dined* with the Duke of Moncrieffe? My word."

"Aye." Logan's eyes glimmered with shared amazement, and for a few treasured seconds, Mairi forgot that he had just rejected her. As he spoke animatedly, she felt the old familiar connection to him and was thrilled to hear about his meeting with the duke.

"You wouldn't have believed it, Mairi, he said, speaking with enthusiasm. "The castle was like a palace, and the plates were trimmed in gold. There were servants with shiny buckled shoes and curly wigs, and the food was...." Suddenly he stopped himself and took a breath. "I'm sorry. Someday, I will tell you everything, but tonight I must return to my men. They are camped not far from here."

"But what about *us*?" Mairi asked, thinking selfishly. "Can't you sleep here with me tonight and see Hamish in the morning? Must you leave so soon?"

"No, Mairi." He bowed his head and shook it. "Perhaps I shouldn't have come. It only makes this harder."

"Makes *what* harder?" she asked with a sickening knot of apprehension in her belly.

His eyes lifted. "The fact that I must say good-bye to you."

By that point, her heart was racing out of control with terror. "What are you saying? For how long?"

"I don't know," he replied. "It depends what happens on the day of the invasion. Surely I don't need to tell you how dangerous it will be. Men will die."

Mairi fought to keep her worries in check and not fall apart completely. "I don't want to lose you."

His eyes darkened with purpose. "Believe me, all I want is to survive so that I can return here and hold you in my arms again. Love you properly."

The mere mention of being held in his arms filled her with anguish and longing. "Please, Logan. Can't someone *else* lead the charge? Why must it be you?"

"Because the men believe in me," he said flatly, gripping the handle of his sword.

Her gaze dipped to his hand upon the large, unfamiliar weapon at his side. She had never seen anything so extravagant before. "Where did you get that? Did the duke give it to you?"

"Nay," he said. "I found it, and it's a special sword, Mairi."

"How so?"

He spoke quietly, almost somberly. "It once belonged to the Butcher of the Highlands."

Mairi's breath caught in her throat. She couldn't quite believe what she was hearing.

"It's part of the reason the men have put their faith in me," Logan continued in a low voice. "Maybe it's superstitious nonsense, but word has spread throughout the Highlands that I am destined to lead this army and drive the English out of Leathan Castle. That I am somehow blessed with the Butcher's strength."

Mairi shook her head frantically. "If the Butcher were blessed, he would still be alive today, but he is *not* here. He is dead, which is exactly where you will end up if you believe you are somehow exalted. You are just a man, Logan—a *great* man—but I have a bad feeling about this. Please do not go. Stay here with me."

She reached out to him, but he quickly moved away. "I have to go."

"No, wait…." She followed him.

"I don't know what will occur when we invade," he said as he made his way around the kitchen table to the door. "If we are successful, I will have avenged my father's death and made things right for the Campbells. Then I will come back for you."

"*If* you are successful...?" Her blood turned to ice in her veins as he opened the door and walked out. She followed him out to the yard where he returned to his horse and gathered up the reins.

"Why did you even bother coming back here?" she asked in a sudden, heated rage. "Clearly all you've ever wanted is vengeance. Why did you let me fall in love with you if you always intended to leave? Did I mean that little to you? Am I not enough?"

He was about to place his boot in the stirrup, but stopped and frowned. He faced her angrily. "You were everything to me, Mairi, and you still are. I came here tonight because I love you and I couldn't go into battle without seeing you one last time."

One last time..."You're breaking my heart, Logan. I cannot do this. I cannot say good-bye to you." She turned to go back into the house, but stopped abruptly on the threshold when he called out to her.

"Please lass, I must have your blessing!"

Oh, God...

The pain in her heart became a fierce, impregnable torment. Tears blinded her eyes. She grabbed hold of the doorjamb to steady herself.

"It will be a bloody battle and many men will perish," he continued. "I do not wish to be one of them, but if that is God's will, I must accept it and hope that I have proved myself worthy." She heard his footfalls across the ground, approaching. "You are the closest thing to an angel I've ever known. Please offer me something, Mairi. Tell me I am doing the right thing."

She covered her face with trembling hands and forced herself to turn around. He was so rugged and handsome in the dim light spilling out from the open door. A suffocating sensation tightened her throat. She had no words. All she could do was run toward him, throw her arms around his neck and hug him tightly. "You must follow your heart, Logan, and if this is what you believe you must do, then do it. Fight, and win. But *live!*"

A tear fell across her cheek. She quickly wiped it away.

Logan cupped her face in his hands and touched his forehead to hers. "Please believe that this is not just about me and my vengeance. It is about you, too, and all the other innocent Scots who suffer at the hands of the English. We must stand up to them, show them that we will not tolerate such brutality— that it's their only hope for a peaceful future."

In that moment, Mairi felt a surge of pride and a love so deep, she could barely keep it from bubbling out of her heart. Rising up on her toes, she pressed her mouth urgently to his. The kiss sent the pit of her stomach into a wild swirl of desperation, for she knew she must make the most of this kiss. Sear it into her memory forever, for it could be their last.

Salty tears trickled down her cheeks as he scooped her into his arms and ravished her mouth with his, ran his hands through her hair and down her back, leaving her mouth and body burning with fire. He planted kisses on her cheeks, neck, and shoulders, crushing her to him while she was forced to endure the unbearable agony of his good-bye.

"I will live," he whispered in her ear, and she shivered with a prayer for the same.

It nearly killed her when he drew himself away. Mairi wiped her tears and steeled herself against the fear and heartache, for there was nothing she could do now but send him off to fight with her blessing, and bear their separation with every ounce of strength she possessed in her soul.

He mounted his horse and sat high in the saddle, gazing down at her in the dark, rolling mist. She strode forward, laid her hand on his muscular thigh, and spoke with passion. "Go and get your castle back, Logan. Avenge your father's death and drive those Redcoats back to England."

Something flashed in Logan's eyes—a mixture of surprise and triumphant exhilaration. His horse took a few restless, impatient steps, and Mairi backed away to give them room to pass.

"Wait for me, Mairi," Logan said. "I will come back for you."

As she watched him gallop away, vanishing like a specter into the mist, she turned her eyes to the overcast night sky and listened to the fading sound of hooves in the distance.

Then there was only silence.

Please, Lord, bring him back to me.

Pray God we don't get buried alive, Logan thought as he wormed his way through the narrow, subterranean passageway that would take him inside the castle walls. He had thought he knew the tunnel like the back of his hand. He had been the one to dig it out, after all—a lifetime ago with his brothers as a punishment for picking on other lads who were smaller and younger than they were. They had been sworn to secrecy about the tunnel, and Logan had never told a living soul. Until now.

But tonight, the tunnel seemed far longer and narrower than he remembered. Though he supposed it was a matter of perspective. He was no longer the lean, willowy lad he had been at the age of ten when he could shimmy through it in twenty seconds flat.

Particles of dirt fell from the earthen ceiling over his head, and he paused with the torch in front of him, squinting upwards to make sure the whole structure wasn't about to collapse on top of him and his men. *Damn*, that would be a sorry conclusion to this campaign. It would spoil their entire battle plan—which involved Logan, Tomas, Fergus and Gawyn making their way through the castle undetected and opening the main gate.

"Are you all right back there?" Logan asked, unable to look over his shoulder.

"I feel like I'm crawling back into my mother's womb," Tomas grunted. "How much further?"

"Not much. It should be just ahead." Sure enough, the narrow tunnel grew wider and Logan was finally able to stand up in a hunched-over position. He held the torch aloft and helped Tomas climb out of the hole. Fergus and Gawyn—two of Angus's most trusted warriors—brought up the rear.

"This is where we will enter," he whispered. "We must remove these stone blocks as quietly as possible, which will bring us into the storage closet in the surgery."

"There should be no one in the closet at this hour," Tomas said, "but we must be very quiet."

"Aye. Let's get busy." Logan passed the torch to Tomas and began to pry the blocks away with his bare hands.

❦

After that, it was a swift and straightforward expedition through the castle in the dead of night. They paused only to silence a few Redcoats who had the bad luck to encounter them in a dark passageway, and tried to sound an alarm.

In relatively short order—thanks to Tomas's excellent sketches of the castle interior, which was vague in Logan's memory—he and the others reached the roof, slayed the guards posted at the battlements, and signaled with waving torches to the surrounding armies in the forest to make their way to the main gate. As soon as they were within view, Logan and his men raised the heavy iron portcullis, which rattled on its chains and finally woke the British soldiers from their slumber.

❦

By the time the British realized that the enemy was charging through the gates, the Campbell and MacDonald armies had reached the barracks with their claymores held high. Terrifying battle cries filled the night, followed by the sounds of musket fire and the clang of steel against steel.

Logan ran across the rooftop to the stairs, burning to join the fight, his blood racing with vigor.

Below, the soldiers scrambled to assemble themselves, but they had no chance in the unexpected frenzy of the attack.

"Wake up, ye bloody bastards!" a MacDonald warrior shouted through the window of the barracks as Logan dashed down the steps and reached the bailey floor. He drew his sword from its scabbard with a tremendous scraping sound that filled him with fiery determination.

"Go back to England where you belong!" he roared as he charged into a disorganized cluster of Redcoats who were fumbling with their muskets. He plunged his blade into the belly of one who was about to fire his pistol into Logan's face. The pistol fired into the air instead, and the soldier fell back.

With a powerful surge of bloodlust, Logan turned just in time to defend himself against an unarmed soldier dressed in nothing but his unmentionables. The soldier cried out with panic and desperation as he lunged at Logan and knocked him onto his back. The wind sailed out of Logan's lungs and his sword fell from his grip. The soldier wrapped his hands around Logan's throat and squeezed. Logan kicked and struggled and gasped for breath. Then suddenly the soldier's expression turned cold, his grip loosened, and he fell forward.

Logan pushed him back, rolled him to the side and saw a knife in his back. Tomas arrived to pull it out. He wiped the bloody blade on the dead man's unmentionables, and re-sheathed it in his boot.

Holding a hand out to Logan, he said, "Get up, ye lazy arse."

Logan picked up his sword and rose to his feet. He was still fighting to catch his breath as another Redcoat came charging toward him with a bayonet.

⪻⪼

Stomach burning with anxiety, Colonel Gregory Chatham sat down on a chair in his quarters and struggled to pull on his boot. "Where the bloody hell is my pistol?" he shouted over his shoulder as Lieutenant Roberts loaded it and handed it to him.

"Thank you…. Dammit! Just set it right there, on the table!" he shouted irritably. "What is wrong with you? Can you not see I don't have a free hand to take it from you?"

Without a word, Roberts set the loaded pistol on the table and returned to the wardrobe to fetch Gregory's jacket. Seconds later, he returned with the garment held out, ready for Gregory to slip his arms into the sleeves.

"This is madness," Gregory said, rising to stand. "What was my father thinking, sending me here to a Scottish castle in the middle of nowhere to fight the Scots? Clearly we are outnumbered here! We are surrounded and out of our depth!"

"It was a surprise attack," Roberts replied as he slid the jacket onto Gregory's shoulders and quickly brushed a hand over the polished epaulettes to wipe away a fleck of dust. "How in the world did they get through the gates? They must have scaled the walls."

"There is no imagining what these savages are capable of. They are like apes."

A sudden pounding at the door caused Gregory to jump. He hurried to button his jacket while Roberts moved to answer the knocking.

"Who is there?"

"It's Captain Jones, sir. There has been an attack!"

Gregory glanced at Roberts with disbelief. "As if we didn't know?"

"A Scottish army has entered through the main gate," Jones continued from outside the door, "and they are fighting our men as we speak! They are Campbells and MacDonalds together!"

"Open the door you fool, and let him in," Gregory said to Roberts.

The next second, Jones was saluting and speaking in a rush of words, almost incoherently, describing gruesome details of what was transpiring in the bailey below. His eyes grew wide with panic. "It's the Butcher!"

Gregory frowned. "What are you talking about? The Butcher is dead!"

"No, sir, he lives!" Jones explained. "He has broken through the gates—he lifted the portcullis with his bare hands!—and he means to kill every last Englishman who crosses his path. He has amassed a giant army, sir, bigger than you can ever imagine, and they outnumber us at least twenty to one. The men need you in the bailey to lead them! There is no time to spare!"

"To lead them in battle?" Gregory replied with horror. "Against the Butcher of the Highlands? Are you mad? It's a lost cause."

Jones's eyebrows pulled together with bewilderment. "It may be sir, but…."

"Do shut up! We cannot possibly win the day under such impossible odds. There is no hope, Captain. You must tell the men to do the best they can and keep fighting. For King and country! All we need is…." He swallowed uneasily. "We need time to raise the white flag of surrender."

"Shall I do that now, sir?" Jones asked.

Gregory considered that for a moment. "No! We cannot give up too soon. We mustn't go down without a fight. Let us press on! Perhaps we can still turn things around. Go back out there and command your men to keep fighting. At any cost. It will strengthen our position in negotiations if we do not back down too quickly."

Captain Jones's eyes filled with a look of disillusionment. "Yes, sir. We will keep fighting until we see your white flag."

"Good man."

Jones left Gregory's quarters.

Gregory shut the door and turned quickly to Roberts. "If it truly is the Butcher of the Highlands out there, there is no hope for anyone. We must leave here, Lieutenant. We must find a way to the stables and mount two horses and escape."

Roberts frowned at him.

"We must survive and reach Edinburgh in order to file a report…and to fight another day," Gregory explained. "Dammit, Roberts, don't look at me like that. Do you want to live, or don't you?"

"I do, Colonel, but shouldn't we raise the white flag?"

Gregory hauled back and smacked Roberts hard across the cheek with the back of his hand. "You know nothing of the Highlands, you bloody fool. If we surrender to the Butcher, we will die, for he is the most savage Scot who ever lived. Every man must fight for his own survival. We must leave here immediately, so that we may report what has occurred and retaliate when we are better able."

"Live to fight another day," Roberts replied despairingly.

"Exactly. Now get me to the stables."

"Yes, sir."

Gregory picked up his pistol and followed Roberts into the corridor.

⚜

Logan dodged the soldier's bayonet charge and grabbed hold of the barrel end of the musket, whirling the man around and swinging him off his feet. The weapon slipped from the soldier's hands, and Logan spun around to point the blade at the man's chest.

"I surrender!" he called out, raising his hands in front of his face. "Please, Butcher, don't kill me! I don't want to die!"

For a few intense, heart-stopping seconds, Logan glared down at the man who just had tried to run him through, and saw nothing but a lad. He couldn't have been more than fourteen.

Logan's heart beat thunderously in his ears, drowning out the sounds of chaos and violence all around him. He stood motionless, arrested on the spot, faltering....

Suddenly, Mairi's face flashed in his mind.

"Hands on your head," Logan commanded. "Get up on your feet and march over to that wall, then get down on your knees."

Logan called out to Tomas who was fighting about twenty paces away. "Tomas! Those who surrender will be taken prisoner!"

"What?" Tomas replied with bewilderment, for that had never been part of their plan.

In that moment, Logan saw a flash of red—two British officers running down the steps toward the stables.

"Sweet Mother of God," Tomas said, witnessing the same thing and finishing off his opponent. "That's Colonel Chatham!"

Chatham and his lieutenant ran into the stables and emerged seconds later, astride two bays.

"*Yah! Yah!*" They galloped headlong toward the open gate.

Logan shouted at the British soldiers who were still fighting. "Look there! Your colonel is deserting you! If you want to live, surrender now! Lay down your weapons and you will be taken prisoner!"

The fighting slowed to a hush as Chatham and his lieutenant galloped across the bridge and disappeared into the night.

For what seemed an eternity, the soldiers of the garrison paused and caught their breath. They glanced around at each other, uncertain what to do.

Then a voice sounded from the far side of the bailey. "*We will never surrender! Keep fighting, men! In the name of King George!*"

"I'll get him," Tomas grumbled. He raced across the blood-soaked ground, leaping over dead bodies along the way, to extinguish the booming voice of the Englishman who had deemed himself their new leader.

Logan turned back to the boy he had just escorted to the wall and felt the breath sail out of his lungs. There was a pressure in Logan's gut, which quickly exploded into a fierce burning. He looked down and saw the handle of a knife sticking out of his belly.

"*Damn...*" he whispered.

The boy who had charged him with the bayonet ran off. Logan turned to watch him, and dropped wearily to his knees.

Just then, the boy was shot in the back. He fell forward in a bungled heap, lifeless on the ground, while Logan gazed down at the blood seeping across his own shirt.

CHAPTER
Twenty-two

Father?

Logan wasn't sure how long he had been lying on his back, staring up at the twinkling stars in the sky. The moon was especially beautiful beyond wispy, floating clouds. All the sounds of battle had faded to nothing.

We did it, Father. The English are beaten and their colonel has fled. The Campbells will soon have their castle back, and your old friend Tomas will be here to guide them.

The pain in Logan's belly melted away. There was only a cool, numbing sensation spreading from his core to all his extremities.

Fitzroy is dead too, and Darach is alive in France. I wrote him a letter. Perhaps he will return one day.

A tingling awareness danced across Logan's flesh and he began to feel cold. He closed his eyes and tried to imagine a hot summer day.

The sun beat down upon him.

Mairi gave him a dazzling smile at the edge of the creek where he once kissed her.

I'm sorry, Mairi. I wanted to come home to you and Hamish, to live a peaceful life. No more killing.

He thought of the boy soldier.

You were right. Killing darkens the soul. And yet....

⌁⌇⌁

Logan heard a voice in the distance.

"Captain Kearney! Do you have the key to the powder magazine? We need only light a fuse!"

Kearney?

Somehow, Logan found the strength to sit up and look around. He saw an officer running across the bailey. "I am on my way!" the man shouted.

No, you are not.

Logan reached for his sword, which lay in the dirt beside him, and wrapped his bloodied hand around the grip.

Captain Kearney arrived at the door to the powder magazine and dug into his pocket to search for a ring of keys, while the other man who had beckoned to him was shot dead beside him. Blood splattered onto Kearney's cheek. He watched the man drop, then fumbled faster to find the key.

Logan stood up and gritted his teeth. He set his feet apart, planted them firmly on the ground, then slowly, carefully, pulled the knife out of his stomach. Blood gushed forth from the open wound, but he ignored the pain as he let the knife fall from his grasp. He focused on Kearney and nothing else.

Logan envisioned what that despicable scoundrel had done to Mairi five years ago. A mixture of white-hot fury and vile, black hatred oozed from his soul. He quickened his pace and reached Captain Kearney just as he was inserting the key into the lock.

"Are you Captain Joseph Kearney?" Logan asked, while the whole world turned red before his eyes. Rage—and a ravenous desire to kill a thousand times over—exploded in his head. He found himself amending a previous thought.

No, Mairi, you were not right. Peace is not for me. I am a warrior. I will kill this man and gladly die a warrior's death.

Captain Kearney, initially distracted by the task of unlocking the door to the powder magazine, turned around. He glanced down at Logan's bloody shirt and the heavy claymore in his hand, which Logan held low at his side, for he did not possess the strength to lift it.

"Yes, I am he," Kearney said. "Who are *you?*"

"The name is Logan Campbell, and you raped my wife."

Kearney's eyes narrowed with derision as he slowly reached for his sword. "I have no idea what wife you are referring to, savage, because I've raped too many Campbells to count."

Just as he drew his blade from the scabbard, Logan pulled his pistol out of his belt and blew a hole in Kearney's guts. Kearney fell lifelessly to the ground.

With a dark satisfaction that bordered strangely on indifference, Logan stepped over him and pulled the armory key out of the lock. He placed it in his sporran for safekeeping. Then he stumbled slowly along the wall, dragging the tip of his sword through the dirt, toward a quiet place in the corner of the bailey, behind two wooden barrels. He used his sword to keep his balance as he lowered himself to his knees. Then he lay down on his back, looked up at the sky again, and listened to the sounds of the night.

The battle was coming to an end. There was no more musket fire. No screams of agony. It was done.

Tomas bellowed from the rooftop. "The castle is ours!"

A cheer rang out from below.

But Logan could not cheer. All he could do was lay quiet and still, wondering if his soul would float to Mairi and stay with her forever on the croft in the glen. Or would he go straight to heaven...or to hell?

Hell, most likely.

"Joseph Kearney is dead," he whispered to Mairi. "He will never lay a hand on you again."

I'm sorry I could not forgive.

He felt a cold shiver run through him. Logan's eyes fell closed. When he opened them a moment later, he was gazing up at the face of a rugged, aging Highlander with a long beard.

"Father...?"

Then Logan was lifted from the ground, and taken away.

Mairi was on her knees at the creek, filling a bucket with water, when she heard the approach of a horse and rider from across the field. Quickly, she got to her feet and set the bucket down on the creek bank. Leaving it there, she gathered her skirts in her fists and ran toward the house.

"Please, Logan, let it be you…."

Her voice faltered and her stomach dropped when she reached the house and saw that it was not her husband trotting into the yard, but a MacDonald warrior she did not recognize, ponying a second riderless horse behind him.

The Scotsman was a large man with freckles, a red beard, and a gruesome-looking scar that ran diagonally across his face from his temple to the bottom of his nose.

"Good morning," he said, sitting high in the saddle, leaning forward over the pommel. "Am I in the right place? Are you Mairi Campbell?"

Isla came out the front door while wiping her hands on a washcloth, and greeted him. "Aye, you're in the right place," she said. "Who are you?"

"The name is Gawyn MacLean. I come with news from Leathan Castle."

"Good Lord," Isla replied. "Come into the house."

Speechless, Mairi stared at the man as he dismounted, for she couldn't seem to think or move beyond the rising tide of apprehension that clouded her thoughts.

Gawyn glanced at her only briefly as he passed by, as if he were hesitant to deliver the message. Her heart throbbed in her chest and she had to fight to keep her emotions in check, for she feared the worst.

She followed him inside and spotted Hamish in the chair by the window darning one of his own stockings—which Isla had insisted he learn how to do. He had poked a hole in it with his big toe.

"Hamish, go outside and fetch the bucket of water I left down at the creek," she said.

Her son gazed with fascination at the monstrous, red-haired warrior who stepped across their threshold. "But ma…."

"No arguments, Hamish. Go *now,* please."

He let out a huff and shuffled dejectedly out of the house.

Gawyn waited for Hamish to go, then turned to Mairi. "I have good news and bad news."

"Start with the good news," Mairi said.

"Right." Gawyn cleared his throat and fidgeted with the tartan that was draped over his shoulder. "The invasion was a success and the Campbells reclaimed the castle. The Redcoats who surrendered were taken to the prison where they are being held until confirmation arrives that the English will not retaliate or try to drive the Campbells out again. What else…?" He paused and searched his mind for the rest of his speech, which it appeared he had rehearsed many times. "Oh yes. Negotiations are taking place as we speak, and we have the support of the Duke of Moncrieffe, who is close to the King. In light of the fact that Colonel Chatham was both a tyrant and deserter, we have every reason to believe that all will work out in our favor and Leathan Castle will be lawfully restored to the Campbell clan."

"What about Logan?" Mairi quickly asked. "Is he all right?"

Gawyn hesitated. A sick feeling crept into Mairi's stomach.

"That's the bad news, lass," Gawyn said. "Logan was gravely wounded during the battle."

"Gravely…"

"Aye. He was stabbed in the belly. They tried to fix him— they had the British army surgeon working on him, but—"

"But *what*?" She stepped forward impatiently.

"When I left, he hadn't regained consciousness and a fever had set in. He was in a bad state, Mairi. He lost a lot of blood, and I suspect the infection has already…." He stopped himself. "Tomas sent me to tell you this because they wish to bury Logan at Leathan, next to his father. Tomas thought you would want to be there."

"Wait a moment…." She shook her head as if to clear it. "You mean to tell me that when you left the castle, he was still alive?"

"Aye lass, but just barely, and that was three days ago. I swear I've been praying for him every step of the way, but I don't want you to get your hopes up. You must prepare yourself."

She blinked a few times, half in a daze.

"I must go there at once," she said, moving to her bedroom to gather up what she would need. "Will you take me?"

"Of course. That's why I'm here, lass. I only wish I had better news for you."

Gawyn remained in the kitchen with Isla who offered him something to eat before they headed out.

Three days later, after a grueling trip across the Highlands with little rest and no time to spare, Mairi and Gawyn reached a crest on the hill overlooking a loch, where they saw, in the distance at last, the impressive stone bastion that had recently been reclaimed by the Campbells.

Mairi had never seen the castle with her own eyes. She had only heard tell of it from Tomas and others. Seeing it now caused a stirring of pride in her, for it was Logan's birthright and her clan's indestructible stronghold in the Highlands. It was doubly gratifying to know that it had been recovered through an alliance with the MacDonalds and even a few MacLeans—all former enemies.

"Let us hurry," she said, kicking in her heels to urge her horse into a gallop along the top of the cliff. "I cannot bear it. What if we are too late?"

"I'll keep praying," Gawyn said as he followed.

 ❁❈❁

The guards patrolling the battlements on the rooftop recognized Gawyn immediately as he and Mairi approached, and the heavy gate lifted. Mairi followed Gawyn across the wooden bridge into the bailey, where she quickly dismounted and asked the groom about Logan. "Do you know if he lives?"

The groom stared at her with wide eyes. "Are you the Butcher's bride?"

Her eyebrows pulled together into a frown and she shook her head agitatedly. "No, I am Mairi Campbell. I am wed to Logan Campbell. Is he alive?"

The groom's cheeks flushed with color as he regarded her uneasily. He pointed toward a set of windows on the second level of the castle, which overlooked the bailey. "Go there," he said. "They will answer your questions."

Mairi handed her horse over to the groom and turned to Gawyn, who merely shrugged. "Let's get ourselves up there," he said.

A moment later, Gawyn was pounding his big fist on the heavy oaken door. "Open up! Is anyone there? It's Gawyn and Mairi!"

The door opened fast, and Mairi found herself gazing up at Tomas.

"Oh, Tomas!" She rose up on her tiptoes and wrapped her arms around his big shoulders.

"My dear, sweet lass. I'm so glad you made it. I wasn't sure what would happen when you learned of Logan's fate."

She stepped back to accept whatever painful truth Tomas was about to deliver. "What do you mean, his *fate*? Am I too late?" Her throat closed up and her eyes filled with tears.

"Nay, lass, you're not. The fever broke two days ago, and he's been cranky as a bear, asking for you every minute since. I thought you'd never get here."

"He is alive?" Mairi gazed up at Tomas with wonder and disbelief. *Am I dreaming?*

"Aye, lass."

Tomas smiled with laughter and her heart burst open with bright and bottomless joy. She covered her mouth with her hands as relief poured through her trembling body. "Thank God!"

"In all my years," Tomas added, "I've never met such a fighter. Come in, come in."

Mairi entered a large room that appeared to be a study of some kind with a desk in front of a window. "Where is he?" she asked.

Tomas pointed. "Through there."

She crossed to a closed door that led to another room beyond, and placed her hand upon the latch.

"But be careful, lass," Tomas warned, following behind her. "He's not fully mended yet. He's still very weak. Go easy on him."

Mairi opened the door to a darkened bedchamber where the curtains were drawn. To her relief, there lay her sleeping husband in an enormous four poster bed…*alive*.

Slowly, with her insides still quaking with elation, she moved across the stone floor to the carpet where she stood at the foot of the bed, staring at her husband as he lay beneath nothing but a thin white sheet.

How could this be possible? How can I be so blessed?

Though he was pallid and gaunt, and there were scrapes and cuts on his face and arms, he had never looked more beautiful to her. His golden hair was splayed out on the pillow and his face was turned to the side. Even beneath the sheet, she could appreciate his tall, muscular form and the irresistible strength of his warrior body.

Suddenly, Logan startled awake and leaned up on his elbows. "Mairi?"

"I am here." She circled around the bed while he regarded her with open-mouthed shock.

"Have I died and gone to heaven?"

"Nay," she said with some concern at his confusion and the dark circles under his eyes. She sat down on the edge of the bed. "You are very much alive, which must be some sort of miracle, for Gawyn told me what happened. Apparently, even the surgeon did not believe you would survive. Yet here you are."

He raised her hand to her lips, closed his eyes and kissed each of her knuckles tenderly. "It is good to see you, Mairi."

"It is good to see you, too," she replied meaningfully. "Perhaps the Butcher's sword did have some magical powers after all. But goodness gracious, please do not go about believing you are invincible. You are lucky to be alive, you know."

He nodded and lay back down on the pillow. "I am more than aware. And here you are, brought to me again, like an angel."

"I am no angel," she scoffed. "If you could have heard me over the past two days, cursing the loathsome man who did this to you…."

"He was just a lad," Logan explained to her. "And he was frightened. He thought I was the Butcher."

She rolled her eyes and labored to speak with humor and lightness, for she wanted to keep Logan's spirits up. "*Everyone* appears to think that. When I rode into the bailey just now, the groom asked me if I was the Butcher's wife. Is that not the most ridiculous thing you've ever heard?"

Logan regarded her with regret, then grimaced in pain and cupped a hand over his wound. "It's not so ridiculous, lass."

She felt a stirring of unease, as if he'd become disconnected from her somehow. That suddenly things had changed and he didn't *want* her here. Or perhaps he was simply keeping something from her which he did not want her to know.

But he needn't keep *anything* from her, because she loved him, no matter what.

"Oh, my darling…." Mairi leaned down to kiss him on the mouth, then she pressed her cheek tightly to his.

"When I was lying on the ground," he said in a low, husky voice, "and I felt the life draining out of me, all I could think about was you, and how I was not the man you wanted me to be."

She sat back and looked him square in the eye, determined to reassure him that he was wrong. "Do not be foolish. You are everything I could ever want."

Logan glanced away, toward the window, and in that moment she realized that he was not seeking reassurance. There was something else visible in his eyes—a look of dread, or perhaps it was pity, as if he were about to break her heart all over again.

"What's going on?" she asked, feeling her stomach muscles clench tight with trepidation.

"There is something you should know, Mairi. About the battle. And about me."

"What is it?"

He took a deep breath and reached for her hand. "There is a reason the men think I am the Butcher, or that I am somehow possessed of his spirit."

"Why is that?"

"Because I was ruthless as we marched across the Highlands and planned our attack. All I wanted was to conquer. And on the night of the invasion, I was without mercy and vicious when the slaughter began. I killed man after man. My body was on fire with a hunger for death and carnage. I hated every living thing that stepped into my path—if it was dressed in a red uniform. It was as if I truly *was* possessed by some sort of demon. But then, something happened...."

Mairi sat forward. "What was that?"

"A soldier tried to spear me with his bayonet."

"Surely he was not the first."

"Nay, and I stopped him as I would any other, but then I saw that he was nothing but a lad, not much older than I was on the battlefield at Sheriffmuir." Logan's eyes met hers. "I should have killed him, Mairi, but he pleaded for his life and something in me couldn't do it. I changed our strategy in that moment and ordered my men to take all those willing to surrender as prisoners instead of killing all."

Mairi regarded him with admiration. "But that is a *good* thing, Logan. You showed mercy and compassion. How can you think I would not love you for that?"

He shook his head with contempt. "I am not finished yet, lass, because the lad whose life I spared was the one who stuck a knife in my belly as soon as my head was turned."

"Oh, God." Mairi covered her mouth with her hand. "He was the one who nearly took your life?"

"Aye," Logan replied. "He stabbed me. Then all I could do was watch him run off and get shot in the back by a stray musket ball. Life seemed rather bleak in that moment."

Mairi swallowed uncomfortably. "But the fact that he died was not your fault."

"Nay, but my change in orders—that we take prisoners—could have lost us the battle if the men lost their focus. When I watched that boy die, I wished I'd simply killed him. I wished I hadn't let down my guard and put all my men at risk. I only did so because I thought of you."

Fear exploded in her heart. "But you weren't wrong to spare him," she argued. "It's not weakness that compels a man to offer mercy to another. It is a sense of humanity."

He shook his head. "In battle, it's pure folly."

Mairi tried to consider this.

"Perhaps so," she replied after a long moment, hoping to find a middle ground somewhere. But it was no easy task when she had spent the past five years teaching herself that all life was precious, that no one deserved to die, no matter what mistakes they had made in the past or how misguided they still were. All men were capable of redemption and could discover how to achieve it, eventually.

But a battlefield....

She could not deny that it was a different situation because of the intention to win at all costs, and because of what was at stake—the need to protect home and hearth and family. She could not pretend to understand or truly know what sort of torment a man must endure in such chaotic and frightening circumstances.

"I did not expect it," Logan said, changing the subject, "but the Campbell clan is calling for me to become their chief."

Her head drew back in surprise. "They are?"

"Aye. They know about what happened at the Battle of Sheriffmuir—I forced Tomas to tell them—but now they believe it was my destiny all along to lay the groundwork for an alliance with the MacDonalds and take up the Butcher's sword. They believe I was removed from that battle fifteen years ago for this purpose alone—to take my father's place and right the wrongs that the English have put upon us."

Mairi stared at her husband with wide eyes. "Do *you* believe this? That it is your destiny to take your father's place and become chief?"

He inclined his head. "I don't know, lass. It's all a bit superstitious, don't you think?"

She let out a breath of relief that he was not entirely swept away by the idea that he was the Butcher, somehow resurrected from the grave.

"That is not all," he continued.

"There is more?" *How could their possibly be more?*

"Aye. I may have showed mercy to that young lad before he decided to dirk me, but I believe you must know the dark truth about me, lass. About the man you married."

"What truth is that?"

He replied without apology or regret. "There was another man I killed after I gave the order to take prisoners, and I took great pleasure in it, for there was nothing but vengeance in my heart at the time. You say I possess a care for humanity, but I didn't then. Not when I killed that other man. In that moment, I was a heartless, cold-blooded monster. I did not hesitate, and I was glad I did it."

Mairi swallowed uneasily. "Who was this man? What did he do to you?"

"Nothing, lass. It was what he did to *you*." Logan paused. "He was Captain Joseph Kearney."

Mairi blinked a few times as a wave of shock moved over her and prickled her skin. "He was here in the castle?"

"Aye. I saw him about to do tremendous harm. He was going to set flame to fuse in the ammunition store room."

"And you killed him? How?"

"I blew a hole in his stomach with a pistol ball. At close range."

Suddenly, Mairi found herself envisioning all the violent, gruesome and vindictive things she had once wanted to do to the man who had violated her. Images flashed in her brain like bright fireworks against a black sky. She had been suppressing those thoughts for so long that her head spun.

Then she felt a swift rush of dark satisfaction—to know that Joseph Kearney had finally met his end, and that it had been a violent and painful one.

"Did you mention me at all?" she asked, not entirely sure why she was asking the question—except that she craved information. She wanted rich and vivid details. She wanted to picture all of it. Every last second. "Did he know why you were shooting him?"

"Aye," Logan replied. "I told him I was there because he raped my wife."

"But did he know it was *me*?"

Logan shook his head, and she found herself vastly disappointed. "He said he raped too many Campbell women to count."

All the breath sailed out of Mairi's lungs, for she had hoped to enjoy her revenge vicariously through Logan. She wanted Kearney to know that this justice—this so-called, eye for an eye—had, in a way, come from *her,* the young woman in the hay field whose innocence he had stolen...whose father he had murdered.

Logan reached for her hand. "I know you've tried to help me see that I can forgive men for the things they do, and choose not to hate, but Mairi...I do not believe I can ever fully lay the past to rest, or love my enemy. I am a warrior and I will always be a warrior. I also mean to become chief, which means that if there are ever any other threats to the Campbell clan, I will raise the Butcher's sword again." He paused and bowed his head, shaking it slowly. "I fear you will not wish to be wed to such a man. That your feelings for me will not be the same."

She looked down at his hand upon hers. She turned it over to run the tip of her finger along the lines of his palm.

"You ask me how I feel, Logan. The truth is, I never imagined I could ever trust a man enough to allow him to love me, yet I trusted *you*. I believed you would never harm me, and you never did. You loved me and you were patient and gentle with your touch. For that I will always be grateful."

She bent forward to lay a kiss on his open palm, and turned his hand over again to examine the scrapes and scabs on his knuckles. There could be no denying that he was a violent man. A warrior, straight to the bone.

"I do not blame you for thinking that I would not want to be with someone who lives a life of violence and killing, but when you told me about Joseph Kearney just now, and how he had raped so many other women, I was glad you did what you did. For how can I not respect and love you for your ability to protect those who cannot protect themselves, and those you love? What you did—this entire battle—was necessary, and you made all the right decisions, Logan. You were even willing to sacrifice your own life. It is no wonder the men look up to you and want you as their leader."

He squeezed her hand in his, urging her to continue. "What are you saying, Mairi?"

She scooted closer so that she could lay her hand on Logan's cheek. "I am saying that I cannot judge you or think less of you for what you did. It was war, and Kearney was Scotland's enemy, in so many ways. You are a warrior, and there will be times when you must raise your sword. It does not make me love you less. It makes me love you more, for I know that, with you, both my heart and body will be safe."

Logan nodded and pulled her into his arms, buried his face in her neck. She felt his lips and hot breath against her flesh as he spoke. "Aye, lass, you will always be safe with me. I would die before I would see you and Hamish harmed."

Overcome with love, she drew back and pressed her lips to his in a passionate kiss of total abandonment. *Ah, the bliss of it*—for she had never imagined she could ever love a man as she loved Logan today, both physically and soulfully. Her body burned with desire for his touch, and she wanted more than anything to make love to him, every day for the rest of their lives.

He tried to sit up and ease her onto her back beside him, but the knife wound held him back.

"*Ach*," he groaned with a mix of soreness and desire. "I wish I was in a better state to love you properly, lass—and Lord knows, not *every* part of me is impaired—but I am badly wounded. This could be the death of me."

She drew back in horror. "Goodness, do not say such a thing! Poor Logan…you are not well and I am tempting you to do something that will no doubt cause you further injury. Tomas would have my hide." She slid along the edge of the bed, just out of reach, and smiled at him. "This is vaguely familiar, you know. It's how we first met—you were wounded then, too. You were completely non-threatening."

Logan lay down on the pillows again and regarded her with amusement and love in his eyes. "Don't rub it in, lass," he said, "and be warned, I will be perfectly well in a day or so, and then I will show you just how dangerous I can be."

She raised an eyebrow. "Is that a promise?"

"Aye," he replied with a devilish grin that aroused her senses and heated her blood.

She reached for his hand and kissed it. "Then I promise to hold you to that, darling husband. Or should I call you 'chief'? Or 'my laird'?"

He thought about that for a moment. "Just call me 'love,' and nothing else."

The bell in the chapel tower began to chime outside the window and Mairi felt a swell of joy in her heart as she lay down on the bed and snuggled close to her husband.

Epilogue

Summer 1735

"I told you, lass, you cannot follow us," Logan whispered to Mairi as he removed the heavy stone block from the wall and set it on the floor inside the storage room. "The tunnel is narrow and you're as big as a barn."

"I beg your pardon?" she replied incredulously, raising the flaming torch over her head.

Hamish, now ten years old and tremendously tall for his age, chuckled. Logan put his hand over the lad's mouth to stifle his laughter.

"And as beautiful as ever," Logan hastily added.

Mairi gave him an unimpressed look of warning. "If you weren't the father of my unborn bairn, I swear I would…Oh, I don't know what I would do."

Hamish fought to squelch his laughter, and Logan elbowed him in the ribs. "Quiet, lad, you're not helping."

"Sorry," Hamish replied, standing up straighter and pressing his lips together tightly.

Mairi smirked. "You both deserve a good thrashing, but I suppose I can forgive you, just this once." She gestured with the torch. "Go ahead, see if you can escape before I change my mind."

They exchanged looks of readiness, then Hamish turned to squeeze through the hole in the wall.

Before Logan followed, he kissed Mairi on the cheek, then bent forward to speak to her large, round belly. "We will be back shortly," he said to his future bairn.

"Take your time," Mairi replied with a laugh.

⋯⟨≋⟩⋯

"Do you understand why I brought you here?" Logan asked Hamish as they stood on the pebbly beach, below the castle walls, looking out at the sparkling, moonlit water.

For the past five years, many nights before bed, Hamish had begged Logan to recount the story of the battle and how he had reclaimed this castle for the Campbells. Logan always told him that he and Tomas had scaled the walls in order to execute a surprise attack. But Hamish was ten years old now, and he was becoming a man. It was time he knew the truth.

"I do," Hamish replied. "You want me to know how to defend Leathan Castle, and how to prevent others from breaching our walls."

Logan rested his hand on Hamish's shoulder. "That's right, lad. One day, you'll be a man and you'll have a wife and children of your own. You'll want to protect them, as I want to protect you and your mother and your two sisters. I've taught you how to use a sword and a musket, so if you keep practicing, you'll have the skills you will need. But this escape route I just showed you is a family secret. Do you understand? The only people in the world who know of it are Tomas and Angus the Lion, who I trust like a father, and two other faithful friends who helped me reclaim this castle. And of course, your uncle Darach, who helped me dig this tunnel many years back, when we were just about your age. So you must never tell anyone about this, unless it is a matter of life or death."

"I promise I will keep the secret," Hamish replied.

"Good lad." Logan squeezed his shoulder, then bent to pick up a flat stone at his feet. He rubbed his thumb over its smooth surface and tested its weight in the palm of his hand. "This should skip well." He offered it to Hamish.

The lad accepted it and examined both sides before hauling back and pitching it fast across the water. It bounced four times, making giant leaps into the air before it splashed into the blue-black depths.

"Will I meet Uncle Darach when he returns?" Hamish asked, turning to face Logan.

"Of course. The King's pardon has finally been delivered, thanks to the Duke of Moncrieffe's persistent appeals. That man never gives up. So Darach and Larena should arrive any day now...with their sons." He grinned at Hamish, whose eyes lit up.

"I cannot wait to have boy cousins," Hamish said. "All I have are sisters."

Logan ruffled Hamish's curly red hair. "You're a lucky lad to have sisters who love you as much as they do. And remember, your cousins may be rambunctious lads, but they are still very young. Ronald is only four and Alec is not yet three."

"I was only five when you first taught me how to hold a sword."

"A stick sword," Logan reminded him. "You may teach them things with sticks, Hamish, not steel. Will you remember that?"

"Aye."

"Good. And maybe the bairn your mother is carrying will be the brother you've always wanted. We'll know in a few weeks. If it's not a fresh-faced little laddie, we'll keep trying," he added with a wink. "Now let's get back before your mother starts to worry."

Together, they climbed high up the steep, rocky slope to the tunnel entrance, which was concealed beneath a tangle of roots and overhanging shrubbery.

⋘⋙

Three weeks later

"He is going to be handsome like you," Mairi said as she sat up against the pillows on their bed, cradling their newborn son in her arms. "And no doubt, a great warrior. Look at those big little hands. His grip strength is impressive, don't you think?"

Positively spellbound by the miracle of his son's birth and his wife's incomparable strength through it all, Logan crawled onto the bed beside her and held out his arm. She snuggled close to rest her cheek against his chest.

Logan placed his finger into his son's palm, and the tiny, pudgy fist curled around it.

All at once, in a tremendous flood of emotion, he felt the same immense joy and love he had felt upon the birth of his first two daughters, proving yet again that Mairi was the wisest woman on earth—for the love that overwhelmed his heart in that moment eclipsed absolutely everything unpleasant in the world.

"You were so right," he said, meeting his wife's lovely, brown-eyed gaze. "When we first met, you told me that it was possible to let go of hate and replace it with love. Loving you has been the greatest gift of my life, Mairi, and now, our children…" Logan could not continue, however, for his throat closed up and tears filled his eyes. He fought to blink them away. "Look what you've done to me, lass. You've turned me into a sentimental fool. Yet another miracle."

"Indeed," Mairi replied with a tender smile as she handed their precious swaddled bundle to Logan. "Here, you hold him now—in your strong and capable hands."

Logan reached out and cradled his son in his arms. For a long while, he and Mairi gazed with wonder at their son's sweet pudgy face and soft little lips.

"What shall we name him?" Mairi asked. "We've discussed a few possibilities, but…."

"How about Angus Duncan Campbell?" Logan suggested. "For all that the great Lion of Kinloch and the Duke of Moncrieffe have done for us."

Mairi adjusted the folds in the swaddling cloth and tucked them away from the child's face. "That is a good strong name," she replied. "It suits him perfectly."

Logan kissed Mairi on the top of her head. "Do you know how much I love you?"

"As much as I love *you*," she replied with openness and affection.

He shook his head in a blissful state of disbelief. "I never imagined happiness like this was possible."

"Nor did I," she said thoughtfully. "Not until I met you, and you fixed everything that was broken inside of me."

"You were perfect then and you are perfect now," he told her, as he watched his son sleep peacefully. "I am the luckiest man on earth."

Together, they lay on the enormous bed, contemplating their blessings, and falling more deeply in love with each other with every passing second.

A short while later, Logan gently handed little Duncan over to Mairi. "Are you ready to let the others in? Your mother and Tomas are waiting, along with Hamish, Darach and Larena."

"Open the door and let them all in," Mairi replied as she tucked a lock of hair behind her ear and sat up straighter against the pillows.

Logan rose from the bed, moved to the door, and opened it. The members of their family were clustered in the corridor, waiting impatiently to come in.

"Finally," Isla said with a smile.

Logan beckoned for them to enter. He stepped aside to allow them to pass, after which a tremendous deluge of cooing and fussing ensued.

Tomas—now Logan's step-father-in-law—strode into the room and patted Logan firmly on the back. "Well done, lad."

"Look at the darling angel!" Isla said as she tiptoed closer to the bed.

Larena, Darach's wife—who was ever so happy to have returned to her home of Leathan Castle, after five years in France with Darach—followed Isla and offered her own congratulations. "He is so beautiful, Mairi. What a darling boy. You did very well."

While the women, Tomas, and Hamish crowded around the bed to fuss over Mairi and the babe, Logan faced his brother in front of the hearth. They regarded each other steadily and with uncertainty for a moment, and then a look of pride washed over Darach's face.

"You also did well, brother," Darach said. "In everything. I have no doubt that if Father were alive today to see all of this, he would be very proud."

Logan listened to the words his brother spoke and felt another rush of strong emotion, for it was what he had yearned to hear all his life—that he had made his father proud.

Though Ronald James Campbell was in heaven now, Logan believed with all his heart that they would meet again one day, and he would not feel ashamed of the life he had led. To the contrary, he would see his father again with a feeling of pride and serenity.

"What about you, Darach?" Logan asked. "We quarreled before we parted five years ago, and though I apologized in writing, I must know, is all truly forgiven?"

Darach rested a hand on Logan's shoulder. "I, too, must ask the same of you, Logan, for I was harsh that night. Of all things for me to do…to break your sword arm. It's a wonder you could forgive *me*."

Logan drew in a deep breath and thought again of all that he had learned from the act of loving his wife. "Time heals all wounds," he softly replied. "All is forgiven."

He held out his hand and Darach shook it, then pulled him close and gave him a brotherly hug.

"Congratulations," Darach said, drawing back. "The bairn is a fine-looking lad. Clearly, he takes after his mother."

Logan stepped back and laughed. "No doubt about it."

Together, they moved to the foot of the bed to join the others in admiring the latest addition to the Campbell clan. Then the nursemaid brought Logan's two young daughters into the room to meet their new brother. They climbed onto the bed with curious looks on their faces.

Logan watched his wife smile dazzlingly and introduce little Duncan to his beloved daughters. In that moment, he felt a wave a joy so profound, it moved him to tears.

Love....

He understood it now, and was at last content in the knowledge that all their lives would be richer for it, and all that was meant to be, would be.

Dear Reader,

Thank you for taking the time to read my latest Highlander historical romance. I hope you enjoyed it. If this is your first time reading one of my Scottish historicals, you might enjoy book one in this series, CAPTURED BY THE HIGHLANDER, where we are first introduced to the Duke of Moncrieffe and the Butcher of the Highlands. Book two, CLAIMED BY THE HIGHLANDER, picks up where that story leaves off with the tale of Angus the Lion—perhaps the most ruthless and seemingly irredeemable character in this series. The third book, SEDUCED BY THE HIGHLANDER, tells the story of Angus's cousin and Laird of War, Lachlan MacDonald, who made a brief appearance in this novel. Lachlan is the most charming and seductive of all my Highlanders—a heartbreaker for sure.

Book four, RETURN OF THE HIGHLANDER, tells the tale of Logan's brother, Darach, and their hostage, Larena Campbell. Logan plays a large role in that novel, which begins shortly after Leathan Castle is overtaken by the English under the command of Gregory Chatham.

As it stands now, this book is the conclusion to my Highlander series. If you enjoyed the series, please consider leaving a review at Goodreads or your favorite online retailer to help others discover it. And please read on for a complete list of my other novels. I have plenty of historical romances available, as well as a stand-alone time travel romance called TAKEN BY THE COWBOY, which is full of fun and adventure.

If you enjoy contemporary novels about real life magic, you might want to check out my *Color of Heaven Series*.

As always, thank you for reading one of my books, and feel free to visit my website at www.juliannemaclean.com for more information about my other titles and my writing life, or to enter my monthly giveaway for an autographed print edition of something from my backlist. While you're there, be sure to sign up for my newsletter to stay informed about special events and new releases. You can also follow me on Facebook and Twitter, or send me a note through my website.

All for now and happy reading!
Julianne

For more information about this book and the author, please visit Julianne's website at www.juliannemaclean.com. While you're there, be sure to sign up for her newsletter to be notified about new releases and special giveaways. You can also contact her directly through the site. She loves to hear from readers. Julianne is also on Facebook and Twitter.

Lady Amelia Templeton would rather die than surrender to a man like Duncan MacLean. He is the fiercest warrior of his clan—her people's sworn enemy—and tonight he is standing over her bed. Eyes blazing, muscles taut, and battle axe gleaming, MacLean has come to kill Amelia's fiancé. But once he sees the lovely, innocent Amelia, he decidees to take her instead…

Stealing the young bride-to-be is the perfect revenge against the man who murdered Duncan's one true love. But Lady Amelia turns out to be more than a pawn of vengeance and war. This brave, beautiful woman touches something deep in Duncan's soul that is even more powerful than a warrior's fury. But when Amelia begins to fall in love with her captor—and surrenders in his arms—the real battle begins…

Book Two

Claimed By The Highlander

NIGHT OF CONQUEST

With his tawny mane, battle-hewn brawn, and ferocious roar, Angus "The Lion" MacDonald is the most fearsome warrior Lady Gwendolen has ever seen—and she is his most glorious conquest. Captured in a surprise attack on her father's castle, Gwendolen is now forced to share her bed with the man who defeated her clan. But, in spite of Angus's overpowering charms, she refuses to surrender her innocence without a fight...

PRISONER OF PASSION

With her stunning beauty, bold defiance, and brazen smile, Gwendolen is the most infuriating woman Angus has ever known—and the most intoxicating. Forcing her to become his bride will unite their two clans as one. But conquering Gwendolen's heart will take all his skills as a lover. Night after night, his touch sets her on fire. Kiss after kiss, his hunger fuels her passion. But, as Gwendolen's body betrays her growing love for Angus, a secret enemy plots to betray them both...

Book Three

Seduced By The Highlander

IN LOVE AND WAR

The fierce and powerful Laird of War, Lachlan MacDonald has conquered so many men on the battlefield—and so many women in the bedroom—that he is virtually undefeated. But one unlucky tryst with a seductive witch has cursed him forever. Now, any women he makes love to will be doomed for eternity...

IN DANGER AND DESIRE

Lady Catherine is a beautiful lass of elite origin—or so she is told. Suffering from amnesia, she is desperate to find the truth about who she really is...or, at the very least, meet someone who inspires an intense memory or emotion. When she first lays eyes on Lachlan MacDonald, Catherine has a sixth sense that he can unlock the key to her past—and maybe even her heart. But how could she know that the passion she ignites in this lusty warrior's heart could consume—and destroy—them both?

Book Four

Return Of The Highlander

A SCOTTISH PRISONER

Nothing means more to Scottish heiress Larena Campbell than saving her father from the gallows. While on an urgent mission to deliver his pardon from the King, she and her English escorts are attacked by a pair of fierce Scottish rebels. When she is dragged unconscious back to the stronghold of Angus the Lion, a powerful and dangerous Scottish laird, she is furious with her captors and determined to escape at any cost...

CAPTOR AND PROTECTOR

Highland scout, Darach MacDonald, is suspicious of the beautiful and defiant heiress who clocked him in the head during the skirmish with the enemy Redcoats. He suspects she will stop at nothing to win her freedom. When he is assigned the task of shepherding the heiress back to her home, he quickly discovers that spending countless nights on the open road with a lassie as temptingly beautiful as Larena Campbell is enough to drive any hot-blooded Scot mad with savage desire. Suddenly he is overcome by a need to claim her as his own, but when they arrive at her father's castle, all may not be what it seems...

Book Five

Taken By The Highlander

A WARRIOR WITH A SECRET

Logan MacDonald, fierce warrior and bold scout for Angus the Lion, hides a shameful secret. When he arrives injured at a crofter's cottage in Campbell territory during a secret mission for his laird, he is immediately suspected of treachery....

A WOMAN WITH A VISION

When Mairi Campbell stumbles across the mysterious wounded Highlander in a moonlit glen—a member of an enemy clan—she is strangely beguiled and cannot resist the desire to unearth the secrets of his darkened soul. Soon, Mairi surrenders to forbidden passion in his bed, which thrusts her into the middle of a war—in a battle for Scottish freedom, and in a battle against the true desires of her heart....

About the Author

Julianne MacLean is a *USA Today* bestselling author of over twenty historical romances, including the Pembroke Palace Series and her popular American Heiress Series with Avon/ Harper Collins. She also writes contemporary mainstream fiction, and *The Color of Heaven* was a *USA Today* bestseller. She is a three-time RITA finalist with Romance Writers of America, and has won numerous awards, including the Booksellers' Best Award, the Book Buyer's Best Award, and a Reviewers' Choice Award from *Romantic Times* for Best Regency Historical of 2005. She lives in Nova Scotia with her husband and daughter, and is a dedicated member of Romance Writers of Atlantic Canada. Please visit Julianne's website at www.juliannemaclean. com for more information about the author and her books, and to subscribe to her email newsletter to stay informed about upcoming releases.

64677746R00137

Made in the USA
Lexington, KY
16 June 2017